Big Shot

NEW YORK TIMES BESTSELLING AUTHORS
CARLY PHILLIPS
ERIKA WILDE

New York Times Bestselling Authors Carly Phillips and
Erika Wilde bring you a new fun, flirty, standalone romance.

Fall in love with your next Book Boyfriend . . .

Wes Sinclair is a notorious heart-breaker, a hot as sin bad
boy with a panty-dropping smile no woman can resist.
Except for his best friend's little sister and business
adversary, Natalie Prescott, who seems immune to his
flirtatious charms. While she's become a permanent fixture
in his dirtiest, most scandalous fantasies, she wants nothing
to do with him, or his seductive promises. Challenge
accepted. His goal? To bring her to her knees, make her
beg, and show her just how good being bad can be.

* * *

Chapter One

WES SINCLAIR TOSSED his cell phone onto his desk, dropped his head into his hands, and pressed the base of his palms against his eyes in a futile attempt to stem the sudden throbbing in his temples. "I can't believe she fucking did it *again*," he muttered irritably to himself.

"*Who* did *what* again?"

The amused voice of Connor Prescott, one of his business partners, only spiked Wes's displeasure. So much for being alone and being able to vent his frustration. Instead, he lowered his hands and glared at his good friend, who was also directly related to the person Wes was currently annoyed with.

He watched as Connor casually sauntered

into the office, the dust on his jeans and boots a good indication that he'd just come in from working on a jobsite. "The *who* is your sister. The *what* is stealing yet another million-dollar listing right out from under me," Wes snapped, even more perturbed that Natalie Prescott could push his buttons more than any other woman ever had, and make him rock hard at the same time.

Not that *she* knew what kind of effect she had on his dick, and she never would. Because one, she was his best friend's little sister and he'd known her most of his life. And two, he'd never give her that kind of leverage or smug satisfaction when they were business adversaries in an industry where any weakness was exploited. And clearly, Natalie had no qualms about playing dirty. This was the third real estate listing she'd yanked right out from under him in the past month, with either client incentives or a higher bid on the property for sale.

Connor sat down in one of the chairs in front of his desk, not bothering to hide the smirk tugging at the corners of his mouth. "What's the matter, Sinclair? Is your ego so fragile that you can't handle a bit of healthy competition from a girl?"

"Fuck you, Prescott." Wes followed that up with a middle-finger salute, which only made his friend laugh. "This has nothing to do with my ego." He had a reputation to uphold as one of the top luxury real estate agents in Chicago, and Natalie was threatening his status. Not to mention his sanity. And okay, his goddamn ego.

He'd worked his ass off the past six years to build Premier Realty into a powerhouse firm along with his three good friends—another real estate broker and two other guys, including Connor, who previously worked construction but now flipped high-end, multimillion-dollar houses under the Premier Realty umbrella. Wes had industry awards to attest to his business acumen, a stable of high-profile clients any broker would envy, and *he* was the one who usually swooped in and snagged properties from unsuspecting real estate agents. And now, one single woman was starting to make him doubt his own abilities.

Wes leaned back in his chair and gave Connor a direct look. "Is your sister trying to prove some kind of point by aggravating the shit out of me like this? By coming in at the last minute with a higher bid that my client can't top on my own fucking listing?"

"I'm sure she is, and it's your own damn fault," his friend said with a shrug. "She *wanted* to work for Premier, remember? I told you she'd be an asset to the firm. But if I remember correctly, you not only said no but set down the gauntlet with an adamant *hell no*."

Wes inwardly winced. He was totally guilty of voting *hell no* on that particular issue, and he'd held firm on his decision despite Connor's strong, valid arguments in Natalie's favor. He'd counter-argued that it wasn't smart to mix family with business, that it was difficult to keep things impartial and make crucial decisions that could affect one family member over the other, that didn't result in hard feelings or resentment all the way around.

Wes knew of companies that had split or gone under because of family disputes, and he'd likened the situation to his parents' divorce. The split between his mother and father hadn't been amicable. Not even a little. The anger and bitterness had caused so much tension between Ethan and Andrea Sinclair that it had forced friends and relatives to choose sides. Lines were drawn, and no matter who was to blame for the dissolution of the marriage—which had been, hands down, Wes's father's fault—his mother had been the one who'd lost the majority of friends they'd made in the twenty-two years they'd been together.

Wes's mother had been devastated by the loss, and because Wes had been so pissed at his father for being such an asshole, the entire situation was contentious at best. There was no repairing the damage Ethan had inflicted on his wife and son and no bridging the gap between two angry families. There was no way that Wes wanted to risk that kind of division in a working environment with his best friends.

In the end, Wes's argument had prevailed, which was a damn good thing because he didn't think Connor would appreciate the other reason he didn't want Natalie around. *Hey, I know we're best friends and all, but I want to fuck your sister, and watching her strut around the office in her tight-ass skirts and fuck-me heels will have me sporting a permanent hard-on and spending the day fantasizing about bending her over my desk for a slow, hard, afternoon screw.* Umm, no. The only thing a filthy confession like that would get Wes was a black eye, or worse, and he wasn't about to risk being castrated by Natalie's protective older brother. He liked that part of his male anatomy way too much.

Bottom line, gorgeous, feisty Natalie Prescott was too much of a distraction to his dick, and having her in his space every day would drive him crazy. It was as simple, and as difficult, as that.

Wes exhaled a harsh breath and rerouted his thoughts back to his conversation with Connor. "Every partner in this company knows the reasons I said no to your sister, and you all agreed to them." Okay, so he'd coerced and pressured the guys a bit to save his own sanity, but in the end, they *had* agreed. "I didn't realize it would cause a fucking vendetta between Natalie and me." Because that's exactly what it felt like.

Connor rubbed his hands down his jean-clad thighs, that small smile tugging at the corners of his mouth again. "It's not about a vendetta or revenge. You know that Natalie just likes a little competition, and she's damn good at selling real estate."

"I'm better," Wes replied, and immediately realized just how juvenile the words sounded after they'd left his mouth. *What was he, in high school?*

"Not lately you aren't," Connor said meaningfully, the smartass tone of his voice indicating he was thoroughly enjoying the fact that his sister was giving Wes a run for the money in the real estate market. "In fact, I'd go so far as to say that if you aren't careful, Natalie is going to surpass your 132 million in sales last year and knock you off your prestigious pedestal for one of Chicago's best of the best brokers."

And she'd no doubt take great fucking delight in taking him down. Being Connor's best friend and growing up around little Natalie Prescott, he'd witnessed just how competitive she could be and how much she liked to win. Especially when it came to *him*. Whether it had been a game of cards or Monopoly with Wes and Connor or racing on their bikes to see who got to the Circle K down the street first, she'd always strived to beat the boys. And when she did, she always made sure to rub Wes's nose in the fact that she'd trumped him.

Now, as adults, the business friction between them was like a tangible thing—*oh, and did he forget to mention the sexual tension they'd both been deliberately skirting for the past few years only added fuel to their rivalry?*—and he needed to figure out a way to diffuse the situation before his stress levels shot through the roof.

"Natalie knocking me off *any* pedestal isn't going to happen," he said confidently.

"Then you'd better step up your game," Connor said, humor lacing his voice. "It would be kind of embarrassing if my sister, who you refused to let work here, kicked your ass and surpassed your sales record."

Wes rolled his shoulders, trying to replace his frustration with a semblance of calm. He glanced at the clock on the wall, relieved to see it was nearly five. God, he needed a drink. A strong one to wash away the sting of defeat of losing his big deal today to Natalie Prescott.

"Want to head out to the Popped Cherry with me and Max for a drink?" Wes asked, inviting Connor to the trendy bar in downtown Chicago that they all liked to frequent.

"Not tonight," he replied with a shake of his head as he stood up. "I've got a dinner meeting at six thirty with the city inspector who's been assigned to the Amber Glen project, and I need to head home to shower and change before I go."

"Better you than me," Wes teased, knowing how boring those kind of dinner engagements could be. "I'll be sure to have a drink for you."

Connor chuckled. "Yeah, you do that."

A few relaxing drinks, and maybe if Wes was lucky, he'd run into one of his occasional hook-ups and forget all about Natalie Prescott.

At least for a few hours, anyway.

Chapter Two

I T WAS DIFFICULT for Wes to forget about his nemesis for an evening when she was at the same bar, celebrating her impressive sale today—the one she'd essentially *stolen* from him. She was with two of her good friends, Heather and Chloe, and the three of them were sitting at a table in a corner, laughing and enjoying a few rounds of drinks. Natalie's back was to him, and while Wes had caught Heather and Chloe casting furtive glances his way, the sexy thief had yet to acknowledge him since he'd arrived with Max almost an hour ago.

Then again, to be fair, he'd deliberately avoided her as well, spending his time mingling with his own friends and chatting with Logan and Tate, the owners of the bar. He'd already caught the eye of a curvy redhead across the way, and he was certain if he approached the woman, the flirtatious invitation he'd seen in her gaze could easily become a sure thing.

Shockingly, his dick wasn't interested in what the redhead was offering, despite his earlier reasons for being here. The problem was, he couldn't stop thinking about, and looking at, Natalie—from the corner of his eye, of course. It didn't matter that he couldn't see what he already knew was a beautiful face, because her backside provided an equally stunning and arousing view. Her long, thick, dark brown hair fell halfway down her back in soft waves, and his gaze traveled all the way south to the heart-shaped ass that sat perched on the barstool. Thanks to the formfitting dark gray skirt she wore, he was able to admire the slight flare to her hips and the rounded curve of her distract-ing bottom. Her long, slender legs were crossed beneath the table, and despite Natalie's known competitive streak, in business she'd always presented herself as a prim and proper good girl.

And he'd be lying if he didn't admit that he'd always found the intriguing mix of her tenacity and softness a huge fucking turn-on.

Aggressive and ambitious in business and sweet and amenable to his dirty demands in the bedroom. Yeah, he liked the way that sounded. The thought of her dropping to her knees in front of him on command made his cock twitch with way too much enthusiasm and interest. Far more than the redhead, or any other woman in the place, had generated tonight.

Of course, Natalie was the only woman in the bar he wouldn't dare touch, no matter how much she tempted him. She was off-limits, forbidden fruit, and all that clichéd crap. But Jesus, if she wasn't his best friend's little sister, he would have already coaxed her into his bed, if only to get her out of his system so he wasn't so damned fixated with what he couldn't have. And since he wasn't used to not getting exactly what he wanted, it only added to her appeal.

"So, we've been here for over an hour," Max, the other broker in the firm, said conversationally as he leaned an arm against the bar, where they were standing at the far end, a beer bottle dangling between his fingers. "How much longer are you going to try and pretend that Natalie, who pretty much crushed you at your own game today, isn't here, too?"

Wes chose to ignore Max's comment about

today's defeat and feigned surprise instead. "She's here? I had no idea."

"I'm going to have to call bullshit on that one," Max said with a knowing laugh. "You do realize that the civil thing for you to do would be to go over there and congratulate her on the Davenport sale today, right?"

"It was *my* goddamn listing," he grumbled irritably. And he preferred not to eat any crow tonight.

"I don't get what the problem is," Max said, studying Wes too intently. "We still made a hefty commission on our end because it *was* our listing."

"I don't like forfeiting *any* of our commission to the competition." He tossed back the last of his drink and set his glass on the countertop with a loud clack.

Max held his gaze. "She didn't *have* to be our competition."

Jesus. Refusing to have this argument for the second time today, Wes decided that playing nice with Natalie would be much safer than Max digging deeper into Wes's true reasons for saying no to her working at Premier Realty.

"Fine. I'll go and congratulate her." He sounded like he wanted to do anything but that.

Max shook his head, clearly trying not to laugh at Wes's poor sportsmanship. "Maybe you ought to have a slice of humble pie before you head over there."

"Don't be an asshole, Maximilian," he said, using his friend's full name, which the other man hated because it sounded too pretentious, and truthfully, Max was anything but pompous or conceited despite coming from an extremely wealthy family.

"Then don't be a fucking pussy," he shot right back. "Seriously, Wes. You've known Natalie most of your life. You're best friends with her brother. You can't let shit like this get in the way of that friendship. For fuck's sake, go and congratulate her, and sound like you mean it."

Wes hated to admit it, but Max was right. He was being ridiculous and overly reactive about the entire situation, especially when Wes reminded himself, once again, that he was the one who'd held firm on the no-mixing-business-with-family rule. Except he couldn't shake the way their last few real estate interactions had felt as though Natalie was deliberately goading him. Maybe if he acted unaffected by it all, she'd back off and she'd stop trying to one-up him. It was certainly worth a shot.

He glanced back over to Natalie just as her two other friends were leaving the table. It appeared they were saying their good-byes, and while Heather and Chloe made their way to the entrance, Natalie remained behind, texting with someone on her cell phone. The perfect opportunity to approach Natalie presented itself while she was alone, maybe even a little more accessible, and there wasn't an audience around to witness their conversation. Which meant no gossip between the three girls when he walked away from the table if he said or did something stupid. Which was always a possibility.

"I'll be right back," Wes said to Max, and after his friend lifted his beer in a silent toast of encouragement, Wes headed over to Natalie's table. Just as he came up behind her, her phone rang and she picked it up with a cheerful, "Hi, Richard."

Shit. Wes came to an abrupt stop and thought about quickly pivoting around before Natalie saw him so he didn't interrupt her conversation, but she turned her head at that same moment and their gazes met, her bright blue eyes widening in surprise when she saw it was him.

"Sorry." He mouthed the words to her, suddenly feeling awkward when moments ago he'd been so confident. "I'll come back when you're off the phone."

She shook her head as she listened to who-ever Richard was—a boyfriend?—talking on the other end of the line, then she pointed at the seat opposite her. "Sit down. I'll just be a sec," she whispered to Wes.

Not wanting to be rude—he was trying to be a nice guy, remember?—Wes slid onto the barstool across from her. As he waited for Natalie to finish her call, he couldn't help but notice how animated she was with this Richard person, how excited her voice was as she spoke to him.

"I know, right?" she exclaimed enthusiasti-cally, and followed that up with a softer, more modest, "Thank you," which turned into a "Yes, we'll definitely have to celebrate," and "That sounds amazing . . ."

After a minute or so, all Wes heard was *blah, blah, blah* as his gaze focused in on her lush mouth and the way her tongue occasionally slipped out to touch her full bottom lip—pink and soft and generous enough to cushion a man's cock as she sucked him off. His groin tightened at the provocative image flitting through his mind, with sweet Natalie Prescott in the starring role of the gorgeous brunette on her knees in front of him, giving Wes the best fucking head he'd ever had.

In reality, she could have been a complete failure at blow jobs—then again, was there really such a thing as a *bad* blow job?—but in his fantasies, she was a porn star pro who swallowed every inch of his cock and moaned for more.

She laughed at something *Richard* said, and Wes issued the other guy a silent *thank you*, since that burst of amusement made Wes the lucky guy who got to watch the slight bounce of her full, perfect tits. She was wearing a white silk blouse, so business-like and demure, but the pearl buttons were unfastened just low enough to give him an occasional glimpse of virginal lace and a small, pretty pink bow pinned to the front of her bra where it dipped into her cleavage. That enticing peek of smooth, creamy breast was like a tease, and it took supreme effort for him to lift his gaze back up to her face.

Her eyes were cast downward as she listened to the guy on the phone, a smile on her lips, and he was grateful that she hadn't caught him blatantly staring at her chest. He didn't need it getting back to Connor that he'd become a pervert where his sister was concerned.

"Richard, I have a colleague waiting to talk to me," Natalie said, clearly cutting the other man short. "How about I call you when I get home in a little while?"

Richard must have agreed, because they said their good-byes and Natalie disconnected the call. She set her phone on the table and sent a brilliant smile Wes's way. The flush of success suffused her cheeks in a warm, pink glow, and she looked as though she was riding a natural high of victory—which Wes fully recognized since it was usually *him* riding that adrenaline rush after a multimillion-dollar sale.

"Hey, Mr. Big Shot," she said, her light, feminine voice threaded with cheerful vindication. The kind that was self-satisfied without being overtly smug, but the intent was definitely there.

Oh, yeah, she was reveling in today's good fortune.

"Hey, Brat-*Gnat*," he replied, purposefully putting a little emphasis on the *g* part of the shortened name, which he'd given her years ago when they were kids and he'd wanted to swat her away like the annoying insect he'd nick-named her after.

"Pesky as a gnat, huh?" She grinned, clearly catching the context of the word he'd used, and wasn't offended in the least. "It's been a while since you've called me that."

"Yeah, well, you've been especially . . . bothersome lately." More like a pain in his ass, but he *was* trying to be cordial.

"Bothersome?" She arched a perfectly shaped brow, which highlighted the amusing gleam in her eyes. "Is that what you call some-one who's beating you at your own game?"

"Bothersome, inconvenient, same thing," he said with a casual shrug, not surprised that verbally sparring with Natalie, mixed in with that sexual awareness neither one of them ever spoke of, made his dick perk up. "Everyone gets a lucky break now and then."

"A lucky break?" she repeated incredulously.

His backhanded praise sparked a flash of irritation in her bright blue eyes, but before she could dole out the comeback he saw forming on her lips, he oh-so-graciously issued the congratulations he'd come over to her table to deliver. "By the way, good job on the Daven-port listing today."

"Thank you," she said, more modestly than he'd anticipated. Then she tipped her head to the side, regarding him with concern. "Did that hurt?"

Confused by her question—because to his knowledge he hadn't suffered any kind of injury recently—he frowned. "Did what hurt?"

She fluttered her lashes at him coquettishly. "You having to admit defeat to little Natalie Prescott."

The little minx. He swallowed the taste of crow rising in his throat and dazzled her with a charming smile instead. "Not at all," he lied, and signaled for the nearby cocktail waitress. "In fact, I'd like to buy you a celebratory drink. What'll you have?"

Surprise lit her pretty blue eyes, and realizing he was being sincere—at least he *looked* the part—she ordered the house specialty, the Popped Cherry, with an extra cherry. He went with the house beer on tap. When their drinks were delivered, he lifted his toward her.

"Congrats on today's sale," he said amicably, and waited until she tapped the rim of her glass to his before adding, "And here's to the last sale that I'm going to let you steal from me."

Before she had the chance to take a sip of her cocktail, she burst out laughing. "*Let me* steal from you?" she asked with amused disbelief. "Are you serious right now, Sinclair?"

He grinned. "Absolutely." Okay, he knew it was impossible to make that kind of guarantee, that she'd never again outbid him on a listing, but it was worth seeing her get all riled up, which also helped to keep their attraction in perspective. "Like I said, everyone gets a lucky break now and then."

She didn't respond immediately and instead took a drink of her creamy, chocolaty concoction, then slowly licked her bottom lip— distracting the hell out of him with that soft, wet tongue. And when he met her gaze and saw the bewitching heat glinting back at him, he realized that had been the minx's intent.

"Maybe you're just getting a little too lax and careless and arrogant, which is fine with me since I'm the one benefitting," she said with a casual shrug of a shoulder.

That quickly, that easily, she'd turned the tables on him. She was provoking him while also making it clear that he'd made a big mistake by not allowing her to work for Premier Realty. He wanted to be irritated with her for calling him lax and careless—he'd cop to being labeled as arrogant because, well, he *was* cocky at times—when he was a businessman who gave every one of his listings one hundred and ten percent of his effort. But that flicker of annoyance that should have burned bright and been aimed straight at Natalie was instead wrapped up in a fog of lust for a woman he couldn't have.

She took another drink of her cocktail, then pulled one of the cherries out of her glass and set it on her tongue. He watched as her lips closed around the fruit, and she plucked it off the stem and chewed as she pushed her glass toward him.

"Would you like my cherry?" she asked, her tone oh-so-innocent while the seductive curve to her lips was anything but angelic. "It's very sweet and juicy."

Somewhere along the way, they'd gone from talking about work to alluding to sex and her goddamn juicy *cherry*, and now he couldn't get *that* dirty image out of his brain, or the thought of what said cherry would taste like on his tongue.

It wasn't the first time Natalie had playfully enticed him. Despite the current frenemy relationship they had going on, she'd flirted with him in varying degrees since she was fifteen. He'd been eighteen that first time, but knowing her since she was five years old, he'd watched her grow from a skinny, awkward tomboy to a beautiful, curvy girl who had starred in his teenage fantasies and was responsible for more than few of his wet dreams. At fifteen, she'd been cute and had worn her infatuation for him on her sleeve. But now, at age twenty-six, she seemed to take great pleasure in toying with him, as if she enjoyed tying him up in fucking knots. As if she was curious to see just how far she could push him before he'd break.

There were times when he'd been so damn close to giving in, but thoughts of his friendship with her brother, and their business partnership, were always like a douse of cold water to bring him back to his senses. It didn't matter that his pulsing dick was begging to taste her cherry, Wes wouldn't touch her with a ten-foot pole, because he was pretty damn sure Connor would use that same pole to shove it up his ass for defiling his sister when Wes was a guy who had a little black book of fuck buddies, and a woman like Natalie did not fall into that category.

Not now. Not ever.

But it didn't stop him from flirting back, because that, at least, was fairly harmless. "I'm sure your cherry is delicious, but I'm going to have to pass." *Unfortunately.*

"Your loss." A smile kicked up the edges of her mouth as she went ahead and ate the second cherry herself, then chased it down with a sip of her cocktail. "You know, you're making it way too easy to *steal* those sales from you. It's like taking candy from a baby."

He nearly choked on a drink of his beer. "I'm making it *easy*?" Was she fucking serious?

She rested her chin in her hand, the impish sparkle in her eyes taunting him. "You know, it's like you've lost your Midas touch. Or maybe you just don't want to admit that I've got more finesse in brokering a deal than you do. I know *that's* got to hurt," she said in a soothing tone that was totally fake.

A muscle in his jaw twitched with the effort it took to hold back his own grin. "I'll never admit it, because there's no way you have more expertise in this luxury real estate market than I do," he countered easily. "This has been my playground for over six years, whereas you're just getting your feet wet. Today's sale was nothing more than you having the right client at the right time with the right property. Pure and simple luck."

She gave her head a small shake. "Don't be such a poor loser, Sinclair." She reached across the table and patted the back of his hand in a placating manner. "Maybe next time you'll manage to come through for your client . . . if I don't sell the listing first."

Next time, there was no fucking way he was going to lose, and he was suddenly willing to gamble his reputation on it just to prove his point. She started to pull her hand back, but he grabbed her delicate wrist to stop her retreat, which caused her lips to part on a startled gasp and her widened gaze to shoot straight up to his. Ahhh, that definitely caught her attention, as well as threw her off guard. And finally gave him the upper hand. Perfect.

"You willing to bet on that, Minx?" he asked, trading in her old nickname for a newer, more appropriate one, considering just how impudent she'd become. He skimmed his thumb across the pulse point on the inside of her wrist and could have sworn he saw her shiver at his sensual touch.

He let go of her hand, and she quickly pulled it back to her side of the table. He saw a glimpse of that heated awareness that always seemed to simmer between them—hotter and brighter now that he'd stoked the fires a bit— but in the next moment, she tossed her hair back and was all sass again.

"So, you want to bet that you'll sell a listing before I do?" she asked, her voice surprisingly steady.

"Yep," he confirmed as he sat back in his chair and rubbed his fingers along the condensation on his bottle of beer. "Unless, of course, you think these recent sales were all just a fluke and you don't want to take that risk."

"You're kidding me, right? The month isn't even over, and I've managed to 'steal' not one, not two, but *three* listings right out from under you," she pointed out, sounding too gleeful with her success. "The way I see things, the odds are quickly stacking in *my* favor, not yours."

Jesus, she was so fucking hot when she was all fired up. And that made him think of all that blazing energy erupting between them in the bedroom. He was certain the push-pull friction they'd been engaging in for years now would coalesce into the wildest, steamiest, tear-each-other's-clothes-off frenemy sex in the history of fucking. Or at least in *his* history of fucking.

Too bad it would be nothing more than a fantasy for his spank bank.

He leaned forward, folded his hands on the table, and did his best to ignore his unruly dick. "Since you're so confident, how about a friendly wager?"

"Friendly?" she reiterated, a doubtful note to her voice.

He nodded. "I'm willing to put aside the fact that we've become adversaries for the sake of the bet, and to prove who deserves to be on top." He let a slow, teasing smile ease up the corners of his mouth. "Which, I have to admit, is my favorite position."

She laughed at his double entendre, but he didn't miss the slight flush rising on her cheeks. "Of course it is, and I'll accept your friendly wager. What are we betting?"

"Anything you want. Nothing is off-limits." He was that confident he was going to win, so it didn't matter to him what was at stake.

She finished the very last of her drink as she considered her options, then pushed her empty glass aside, lifted her chin determinedly, and met his gaze. "If I win, I want to work at Premier Realty, and not as a menial agent but a broker just like you and Max."

Wes was impressed, and not at all surprised by her request. She was going for the brass ring, the one thing she'd been denied, and topping that off with an even bigger requirement that she be hired on at the same level as himself and Max. Clearly, she was testing him, and expected him to backpedal, but he wasn't at all nervous. In fact, her demand gave him even more of an impetus to win.

"Okay," he agreed, and bit back a laugh at the noticeable shock that chased across her beautiful features.

"You're *that* sure of yourself, huh?"

He nodded. "I'm one hundred percent sure that I'm going to win, so it doesn't matter what you're wagering."

She rolled her eyes at him. "Yeah, you keep telling yourself that. What do you want *if* you win? And you and I both know that's a *big* if."

He steepled his hands in front of him as he thought about his request. There wasn't really anything he wanted, at least not in the ambitious sense of what Natalie had just wagered. So, instead, he conjured up something that would be fun for him but not so much for her. Something that would put her at the mercy of his demands—not sexually, of course—but in a way that would humble her a bit, antagonize her a whole lot, and remind her who was in charge.

After a few silent moments, she narrowed her gaze at him. "What's with that devious look in your eyes, Wes?" she asked suspiciously. "It reminds me of when we were kids and you were planning some kind of let's-torture-Natalie scheme, which *never* turned out well for me."

He chuckled. "Because that's exactly what I have in mind. *When* I win, I want you at my beck and call for two weeks. Whatever I want or need, no matter when I ask, you'll do it without complaint."

Chapter Three

NATALIE SAT BACK in her chair, unable to believe the words that had just come out of Wes's mouth. Somehow, she managed to keep her face carefully composed, but her chest rose and fell a little faster as she tried to process what he'd just anted up for their bet.

Whatever I want or need, no matter when I ask, you'll do it without complaint.

Wow. Her mind conjured up some pretty steamy scenarios, which wasn't difficult to do considering she'd spent most of her youth, and even a few years into her twenties, imagining what it would be like to have all that sexual energy and confidence turned her way. Oh, who was she kidding? She *still* fantasized about how it would feel to have his hands sliding across her breasts and between her thighs, followed by his full, sensual lips traveling that same path. She'd dreamed about his soft tongue pleasuring her until she moaned and writhed in pleasure, and envisioned him pinning her to the bed while filling her full in one deliciously hard thrust.

Jesus. Now was not the time or place to conjure up those arousing thoughts. Heat suffused her entire body, and she shifted in her chair, hoping that Wes mistook her squirming for unease because of his wager.

Then again, it wasn't as if he'd ever touch her the way she'd imagined too many times to count. For as much as they'd flirted and teased over the years—except for that year and a half she'd wasted on her ex, Mitch—Wes had long ago drawn an invisible line that he'd never crossed, then had gone on to build an impenetrable stone wall between them that fateful day when she'd stopped by the Premier Realty office to talk to her brother, and instead she'd overheard Wes's unmistakable voice saying to Connor, *Hell, no. We're not hiring your Goddamn sister.*

She hadn't quite reached Connor's office at that point, and she didn't bother to stick around and hear what else might have been said because it didn't matter. She'd been devastated since she knew she'd be a good fit for the firm and wanted to be a part of its growth, and she'd tried not to wince when Connor called her a few hours later to tell her that it was best if the company didn't mix business with family.

She'd played it off as if she didn't care, but that rejection, coming on the heels of her humiliating breakup with Mitch, had lit a fire under her feet. That had been almost six months ago, and she might have been just starting out as a real estate agent, but since that day, she'd hustled her ass off. She'd been dedicated to building her career and proving to Wes what a big, fat, huge mistake he'd made by discounting her ability to be an asset to Premier Realty.

She'd known Wes for much too long, and he'd been best friends with her brother, Connor, for too many years for her to hold a grudge or allow her resentment to make things awkward between them. Instead, she'd put her big-girl panties on and she'd channeled her hurt feelings in a much more positive direction. She wasn't the kind of woman who got mad. But she was the type to get even.

And with this bet, he'd thrown down the

challenge she'd been waiting for, along with the chance to make him eat his words and regret not making her part of the Premier Realty team. She planned to win, which meant Wes would have to put *his* big-boy jock strap on and welcome her into the fold.

And if she didn't win . . . well, she'd recently been contacted by a recruiter who'd been trying to woo her into taking a job with a high-profile real estate firm in Atlanta. She'd definitely entertained the offer. It would be a fresh start after Mitch, as well as the next step up on her career ladder. The biggest factors holding her back from accepting the job were leaving her family and moving to a new city where she didn't know anyone.

"What's the matter? Having second thoughts?"

Wes's amused voice, which was just shy of being smug, pulled her back to the present. She wasn't afraid to take his dare. In fact, she couldn't wait to get started.

"Not at all, Big Shot," she said, meeting his gaze across the table. "But I would like to clarify your wager. When you say you want me to do whatever you want or need, whenever you ask, are you propositioning me?" Not that it mattered, since he was going to lose the bet, which would make accepting the recruiter's offer a moot point. But she was curious to know what he'd meant by his statement and if he was actually suggesting they finally do something about the undeniable attraction between them that he'd spent his adult life trying to pretend didn't exist—even though she'd seen enough evidence to the contrary.

He slowly shook his head. "Not sexually."

Bummer. A traitorous part of her—mainly, her damn neglected vagina—was disappointed with his answer. She crossed her legs beneath the table. "So, you'd want me to be your slave?" she asked incredulously.

Finishing the last drink of his beer, he pushed his glass aside. "*Slave* is such a harsh term." He contemplated for a moment before a sly smile eased up the corner of his mouth. "Think of it as you being my personal assistant."

She could only imagine the things he'd order her to do. Based on their childhood and the various torture tactics he and Connor enjoyed inflicting and the crazy things they'd dare her to do—which she'd done because she'd pathetically wanted to hang out with them—she was fairly certain he'd make her life a living hell for two weeks. Just because he could.

The cocktail waitress came up to their table to see if they wanted another drink, and they both declined. Before she could walk away, Wes stopped the other woman.

"Hang on, Tricia," he said, taking his wallet out of his pocket. "Let me give you my card and you can close out my tab, along with her drink." He handed over his American Express and gave Tricia a sexy wink that made her blush.

"Sure thing, Wes," she said with a flirty smile.

Natalie wasn't all that surprised he was on a first-name basis with the cute, perky server. He'd probably already gone out with her, because it was certainly his MO when it came to the fairer sex. He loved women, they adored him in return, but he was a serial dater, and most women didn't care because the guy was ridiculously good-looking and hot as fuck. He was a shameless flirt. An unapologetic player. He was a man who'd never, to her knowledge, had a long-term serious relationship with a woman.

But did she mention that he *was drop-dead gorgeous,* which negated most of his more obvious flaws and his inability to commit to anything other than Premier Realty? His masculine features were chiseled to *GQ* standards, and the dark scruff along his jaw only made him look more attractive—and made her wonder, on more than one occasion, how that stubble would feel abrading her neck or the more sensitive skin along her inner thighs. His jet-black hair always had that slightly tousled look to it that was sexy, not messy, and a woman could literally drown in his mesmerizing blue eyes. She couldn't deny that she'd been under the spell of that smoldering gaze a time or two herself, so she knew how potent it actually could be.

Around the age of sixteen, a wild and rebellious Wes quickly learned the power of a slow, sultry, panty-dropping smile that got him laid on a regular basis—which Natalie knew because she'd shamelessly eavesdropped on the many bragging and comparison sessions he'd had with Connor about the girls who'd put out at school. Over the years, she'd seen him use that sexy-as-sin, swoon-worthy smile on whatever woman he'd set his sights on.

Natalie had never been the kind of girl to shed her underwear for just any guy, but that sex-clenching smile of Wes's . . . Jesus, it made her wet, every . . . single . . . time. And when Wes glanced at her after Tricia left the table, her body reacted to the residual effects of the charming, irresistible, half-hitched smile still tugging at his lips, and the goddamn *smolder* that would give Flynn Rider, from the Disney movie *Tangled*, a run for his money in a smoldering contest. There was no denying the slick moisture coating the silky thong between her legs or the needy ache that was totally inconvenient and impossible to ignore.

Good God, she needed to get laid. Badly.

"What will it be, Natalie?" Wes prompted. "Deal or no deal?"

Only one option existed for her. "I agree to your wager, so it looks like we have ourselves a bet. When do you want to start?"

"Right now."

"Okay." The sooner, the better, in her opinion. "Do you have a listing in mind?"

"No. Go on to the Premier Realty app and you pick the property you think you can sell before I do." He gave her a slow, arrogant grin. "That way *you'll* feel comfortable with the price range."

She bristled at his implied suggestion that

CARLY PHILLIPS & ERIKA WILDE

she needed an easy listing to win. "I don't want any kind of special advantage over the competition," she said, her voice terse with annoyance. "That defeats the whole purpose of this bet."

He casually shrugged a shoulder. "Just trying to be a nice guy."

Yeah, right. She rolled her eyes at him as she picked up her phone and opened the app, then went straight for the listings that were over a million dollars. While she'd built a solid client base and equally impressive connections within the realty business, Natalie knew she didn't have a stable of buyers for a three-million-dollar home *yet.* She didn't want her choice to be an easy transaction—what was the challenge in that?—which meant choosing a listing that was higher than anything she'd managed to sell thus far.

Tricia came by with Wes's receipt to sign, and while they chitchatted—or rather, flirted— Natalie tuned them out to concentrate on finding just the right property. She stopped scrolling when she came across a house in Lincoln Park. A residential dwelling with four bedrooms, two and a half baths, and twenty-eight hundred square feet. The market price had been set at one-point-six million. It was a nice family home in a great neighborhood with excellent schools, which made it more appealing for buyers with kids.

As soon as Tricia moved on to another table, she handed Wes her cell phone so he could see the house she'd chosen. "Let's go with that listing on Magnolia Avenue."

His brows rose over those dark, dreamy eyes. "Are you sure you want to pick that property? That listing is quite a bit above your current average sell-through."

He was clearly provoking her, and it only made her more determined to show him just how much he underestimated her ability to find a buyer for the high-end residence. "Yep, I'm absolutely sure. Go big or go home, right?"

He laughed, the deep sound making her insides shiver and her nipples tighten oh-so-traitorously.

"All right, then," he said, a gleam of anticipation in his eyes. "May the best Realtor win."

Chapter Four

EARLY THE NEXT morning—hump day Wednesday—Natalie walked into the Espresso Shot, a small locally owned coffeehouse located in downtown Chicago that was nestled on a side street between corporate highrises. The place was mid-size compared to the bigger coffee giant that was found on every corner, but the coffee and espresso here was the absolute best, in her opinion—smooth with just a hint of nutty and sweet, unlike the strong and bitter brew that most other businessmen and women in the area seemed to gravitate to.

She took her place in line, and even though there was a steady stream of customers who frequented the cafe, it was fairly quiet, which also appealed to her. She enjoyed drinking her latte at leisure while scrolling through her phone for industry news and checking the real estate section in the *Chicago Tribune* to keep abreast of the market. She also made her to-do list for the day, jotted down calls she needed to make, and checked her calendar for any scheduled meetings.

Today, however, was all about strategizing with her co-worker, Richard, who was also an agent at her Maxwell Real Estate office. The company they worked for was one of those franchises, a conglomerate of more than a hundred offices located throughout the country. And because Maxwell was a franchise, there was a business model to follow and corporate bullshit to put up with and hard-line quotas to make or risk being replaced. Which was another reason the Atlanta offer sounded so appealing.

Because of overhead costs, her commission was a few percentages lower than what a privately owned company like Premier Realty could offer, and some days—okay, most days—she felt like she was just a cog in the wheel of the giant corporation. Before becoming a real estate agent, she'd worked for a mortgage company as first a loan originator, then had been promoted to escrow officer. At the time,

Maxwell had been a good place for her to make the transition to realtor, where she could learn the ropes and get her feet wet, and she'd hit the ground running . . . and selling. The experience, at least, had been invaluable.

Right after her change in job a year ago, Mitch had complained about her being way too ambitious, which had translated to him not being the center of her attention as much as he once had been when she worked a regular nine-to-five job. So when her brother, Connor, had caught Mitch cheating on Natalie with another woman, Mitch hadn't hesitated to blame *her* for the affair. According to him, she was never around, she was always distracted by work, and he'd felt neglected. *Poor fucking baby.*

Realistically, Natalie knew she wasn't at fault for his wandering dick, but his betrayal had been like a kick in the gut because they'd talked about marriage and eventually having a family, which was what she ultimately wanted. Yes, she was ambitious and goal-minded, but working hard had been all about building a future and a career, not just for herself but for *them*, so they could buy a house they loved without being financially strapped, and she could take time off to have kids when the time came without worrying about money.

After being with Mitch for a year and a half in what she believed was a committed relationship, she would have thought that he'd be man enough to talk to her about the issues he had with her career or whatever "needs" weren't being met to his satisfaction. If he'd been that unhappy, he should have broken things off with her instead of fucking another woman on the side for the last three months they'd been together while still sleeping in *her* bed. Who knew how long he would have cheated on her if Connor hadn't caught him feeling up a woman in a bar who clearly wasn't his girlfriend.

Enough time had passed for her to think of Mitch as an asshole and a whiny man-child, and while her brain knew she was better off without him and his womanizing ways, at the time, his deceit had been a blow to her self-esteem and had definitely made her more cautious where men and her heart were concerned. Did she still believe in love? Absolutely. One day, she wanted the kind of passionate marriage her parents had, even after thirty-one years together.

So, in the meantime, while she was waiting for her Prince Charming to arrive and sweep her off her feet—which could be months or it could be years—it made sense to focus on her career. There was no telling how long it would take to find a guy who was secure enough in his own masculinity and career that he didn't feel threatened by her being a strong, successful woman in her own right.

Now, after a year of experience with Maxwell Real Estate, she was ready to dive into deeper waters. She was tired of treading her way through the shallow end of the company pool and getting overlooked, despite her recent successes. Selling the listing she'd chosen for her bet with Wes would not only be a really nice feather in her cap but would justify all her hard work the past year. Oh, and it would also get her hired on at Premier Realty, she thought with a smile, which was her end goal, after all.

She took another step forward toward the barista taking orders and glanced around the cafe. Finding Richard sitting in a cozy nook area with two overstuffed chairs next to each other, she gave him a quick wave to let him know she'd arrived and would be right over. The customer in front of her moved away from the register with his pastry bag and hot coffee, and Natalie took the guy's place.

"Hey, Penny," she said, greeting the younger girl who worked most mornings at the coffeehouse. "I'll take my regular."

"You got it," Penny replied as she rang up her order. "A medium vanilla latte and a lemon scone coming right up."

Natalie paid for her morning indulgence, dropped a generous tip in the jar on the counter, and a few minutes later, with her breakfast in hand, she was heading toward the quiet alcove where Richard was waiting for her. He had his laptop open in front of him, and he was staring at the screen while he drank from his paper cup with the Espresso Shot's logo on it.

She parked herself in the chair beside his and set her purse on the ground by her feet and her beverage and scone on the table between them. Since she was wearing an above-the-knee brown fitted skirt, she crossed her legs to keep the material from riding up on her thighs, then glanced over at her colleague, who still had his eyes on his computer screen.

"Anything interesting happening this morning in the industry?" she asked as she reached for her latte and took a drink of the warmed milk, espresso, and vanilla flavoring.

He finally turned his head to look at her, his

light green eyes peering at her from behind a pair of black-framed designer glasses that made him look incredibly sexy. Especially when paired with his fitted navy suit and silk tie.

"Nothing earth-shattering," he said with a grin that revealed perfectly straight white teeth. "But it's early yet."

"So true." In this business, things could change on a dime, but she enjoyed that spontaneous aspect of her job. Every day was a different adventure. Sometimes exciting, sometimes frustrating, but always exhilarating.

"So, you ready to put a game plan together to take down Mr. Big Shot?" he asked with enthusiasm.

She returned his grin as she broke off the corner of her lemon scone. "Let me enjoy my breakfast before I have to think about my nemesis."

Richard chuckled and went back to whatever he was doing on his laptop, giving her a few minutes to finish her latte and biscuit before they talked business.

Last night when she'd gotten home from the Popped Cherry, she'd called Richard as she'd promised she would and told him all about the bet. Her co-worker had started at

Maxwell right around the same time she had, and they'd formed a close friendship. He was apprised of her antagonistic relationship with Wes because Richard was always the one who seemed to get the brunt of her rants about something Wes had said or done to annoy her.

Natalie had plenty of girlfriends, but Richard was her best guy friend. They met in the mornings for coffee, hung out together after work quite a bit, and had even gone to dinner and movies together a few times. He was gorgeous and charming and currently single. He was a good listener, as well as funny and supportive, and he even brought her chocolate cake when she was moody and it was that time of the month.

The man was perfect boyfriend material for any woman . . . except for the fact that he was one hundred percent gay. To look at him—from the sharp, impeccable way he dressed to the deep, rich timbre of his voice, to his very masculine mannerism—he was all male. It cracked Natalie up the way women fawned over him, outright propositioned him, and even sent appreciative glances and smiles his way, which he always handled tactfully.

He didn't openly broadcast his sexual orientation, but neither did he purposely hide it. But sometimes, when he really wasn't in the mood to fend off female attention at a business mixer or company function, she'd attend as his date— i.e., his beard. That's what she enjoyed the most about their relationship, that there was no pressure or expectations. Just a solid friendship that worked for both of them.

She finished off her lemon scone, took another drink of her latte, then retrieved her iPad from her oversized purse that Richard always joked could carry around a small country. She turned the tablet on and pulled up the notes she'd made last night before going to bed. She had no intentions of letting Richard do any of her legwork on this listing—she wanted to win this bet on her own merit—but she was grateful to have someone to brainstorm ideas with.

"Okay, here's what I've got," she said, starting at the top of her to-do list for the day. "First thing this morning, before I head into the office, I'm going to the Magnolia house to do a walk-through. I already looked up everything I could about the property online, but I want to see it for myself so I'll have solid facts and information about the home, the floor plan, and the general neighborhood."

"Good idea," Richard agreed as he closed his own laptop to give their conversation his full attention. "I'll go with you if you'd like."

They often did walk-throughs together, and having a second pair of eyes was always great in case she needed insight or feedback. It would also be helpful to discuss different ways to present the listing to a potential client that would make it more appealing. "That would be great. Once I get back to the office, I want to reach out to that relocation company guy who gave me his business card at a function last week, and see if he has any prospects for a buyer who's looking for a one-point-six-million-dollar home."

Richard made a few other suggestions of leads she could follow, which Natalie added to her growing list. They spent the next forty-five minutes generating creative ways to reach the kind of buyer she needed, and where it was best to concentrate her efforts and resources in order to keep focused on her objective. Which was basically selling the property before Wes did.

By the time they were done, she was energized and excited and ready to get started. She had a solid plan she was ready to execute. As she powered down her iPad and started cleaning up the table between them, she saw Richard look toward the order area of the Espresso Shot, then do a quick double-take. She didn't think much of it and figured some hot guy had caught his eye. Especially when she saw the slow smile ease across Richard's lips.

"Hey, isn't that Wes Sinclair over there, flirting with the barista?" he asked.

Without her consent, Natalie's stomach fluttered like an infatuated schoolgirl's. God, she hated that the mere mention of her nemesis's name had the power to elicit such a spontaneous response inside of her. Tamping down the annoying sensation in her belly, she followed Richard's line of vision and realized by the gorgeous profile of the man's face that it was, indeed, Wes standing at the register placing his order. And judging by the swoony look on Penny's face, he was pouring on the charm.

"Why is he here?" she muttered, not at all happy to have him invading *her* place, especially when she was strategizing ways to take him down. "He never comes to this coffeehouse." Or at least not in the morning hours when she was there.

"Does it really matter?" Richard asked, a

teasing inflection in his voice as he adjusted his glasses on the bridge of his nose. "There is something so damn hot about a guy in a suit, and he knows how to fill his out like it was custom-made for that rock-hard body."

She almost laughed at the wistful sound of Richard's voice. "It probably was." From the impeccable cut of the jacket that silhouetted his frame to the expensive, premium fabric, Wes's attire definitely had that tailored look to it.

"You have to admit, he's exceptional eye candy," Richard said appreciatively.

She couldn't argue with that, so she didn't confirm or deny. No sense in implicating herself either way.

A few short minutes later, Wes collected his drink, then started for the door without noticing her. Natalie held her breath, and just when she thought she was in the clear, he casually glanced her way. Seeing her, he came to an abrupt stop, that gorgeous head of his tipping in surprise as his gaze met hers. She mentally willed him to leave her alone, but knew it was a futile wish when it came to Wes. Not when the opportunity to torment her in any way, shape, or form presented itself.

"Uh-oh," Richard said beneath his breath.

"Here comes trouble."

"You have no idea," she replied through tight lips, her heart beating faster with every self-assured step he took toward her.

Richard chuckled, low and deep. "Yeah, judging by the smirk on his handsome face, I think I do have some kind of an idea of how much trouble he can be."

Wes finally reached where they were sitting, but before he could say anything, Natalie decided to speak first. "What are you doing here?" *Crap.* She hadn't meant to sound so suspicious of his motives.

He heard it, too, and his striking blue eyes glimmered with amusement. "Don't worry, I'm not stalking you or trying to learn all your secret plans for the Magnolia listing. I have a meeting across the street with a client. I saw this place and thought I'd give it a try. It's pretty good coffee," he said, taking a drink from his cup.

His reasoning sounded plausible enough, but she hoped he didn't make a regular habit of stopping in. This was her little space in the morning, and she didn't want to share it with him, not when he was so irritating and distracting. "Richard and I were just getting ready to leave. We have somewhere we need to be." *Now go away so I can think and breathe without inhaling your intoxicating cologne that makes me want to bury my face against your warm neck and get high on your scent.*

At the mention of another man's name, Wes's gaze shifted to where Richard was sitting in the chair beside hers, his gaze narrowing slightly. Obviously, he hadn't realized she was there with someone else and had thought that Richard was a stranger enjoying his morning coffee, like most everyone else in the place. Wes's relaxed posture suddenly stiffened, and he studied Richard intently, as if he were sizing up the competition, which was a completely ridiculous thought to even cross her mind.

She opened her mouth to introduce the two of them, but Richard was quicker. He stood up and extended his hand toward Wes. "I'm Richard Weller, and you're Wes Sinclair, right?"

Wes's brows furrowed even further. "Yes."

The two men shook hands, and Natalie was fascinated by the extra-firm grip Wes seemed to have around Richard's palm before he let go.

"Do we know one another?" Wes asked gruffly.

Richard slid his hands into the front pockets of his pants and nodded. "We met a few months ago at a seminar for short sales and foreclosures. I also work with Natalie at Maxwell Real Estate."

The disgruntled look on Wes's face didn't dissipate until he finally glanced back at Natalie. Then, it gradually dissolved into something more neutral. She wasn't sure what to make of his odd behavior, but it was time for her to go, and she stood up, too.

"You have a meeting to get to, and I have a bet to win," she said, keeping her tone light and cheeky. "So, I guess I'll see you later, Big Shot."

One of his dark brows rose, and the slow, infuriatingly sexy smile curving the corners of his full lips made her toes curl in her pumps. "Yes, I'll definitely see you later, Minx. As for the bet, may the best Realtor win."

"I will," she said impudently.

He laughed, the low, husky sound adding to the tickling sensation in her belly. "We'll see."

He nodded at Richard, then turned and walked back toward the entrance.

Once he was gone, Richard glanced at her with a wicked grin. "God, Mr. Big Shot really is a hot piece of ass."

"No," she disagreed. "Most of the time he's just an ass, nothing hot about it."

Richard put his computer into his leather laptop bag, his gaze way too perceptive. "Yeah, you keep telling yourself that, *Minx*."

Her face warmed at the nickname Wes had recently given her, which she secretly loved but would never admit to it. "Keep telling myself what?" she asked, wondering what her friend was getting at.

"That the two of you aren't hot for each other," he said blatantly. "You guys act like you're frenemies, but take it from an outsider who just saw the two of you engage in the equivalent of verbal foreplay."

"We did not," she refuted. *But yeah, they kinda did.*

Richard rolled his eyes. "And did you not see the way he checked me out when you introduced me? And it wasn't because *I'm* hot and he wanted to get into my pants. He was sizing up the competition. I think Wes thinks that we are, *you know*." He waggled his brows for comic relief.

It worked. She burst out laughing, because the idea of her and Richard sleeping together was absurd. The man wanted nothing to do with breasts and vaginas.

"Not to mention the way he looked at you,

as if he was thinking of all the dirty things he wanted to do if he had the chance to get you naked."

For a few moments, before Wes had realized that Richard was with her, she *had* felt the heat of his stare—the way his gaze had leisurely dropped to her lips, then to her chest, making her body ache in inappropriate places. "It's nothing," she muttered, and turned away from Richard as she shoved her iPad into her purse.

"Oh, it's something, sweetheart," he said, sounding more sincere now. "But you obviously don't want to admit it."

Not out loud, anyway. Their attraction was just all part of that frustrating push-pull between them, that back-and-forth verbal foreplay that Richard had pointed out. It had never amounted to anything and never would, because Wes seemed to have a *no fraternizing with his best friend's little sister* rule that he strictly abided by.

Which was probably a good thing, considering what a player and notorious heartbreaker Wes was when it came to women. She'd already had her heart shattered once, and she was *finally* in a good, solid place emotionally. Given the goals she had in life that included a husband and kids, Wes Sinclair, playboy extraordinaire, did not fit the bill, and she'd be an idiot to get involved with another man who didn't share her views.

Chapter Five

NATALIE GLANCED FROM her cell phone to Richard, who was leaning a hip against her desk in her small cubicle that was her "office" at work. His arms were folded across his chest as she waited in nervous anticipation for a return call from Max at Premier Realty, who'd agreed to be the selling broker and mediator between her and Wes on the Magnolia listing to keep the bet fair.

"I can't believe it's come down to this," she said, trying to calm the jitters in her stomach.

"It's not over until it's over," Richard said, trying to be supportive.

Since she and Wes had made the bet, it had taken her five days of major hustling, dozens of cold calls, and pounding the payment before she'd gotten a solid lead from the relocation company. They had just signed on a new client, a neurosurgeon, who was transferring from Pittsburgh to Chicago with his wife and three children and were looking for a new residence. Their criteria had matched the Magnolia listing, and after flying into Chicago to walk through the house, the Sandersons had fallen in love with the property.

Unfortunately, Wes had a client who was equally enamored of the home.

First thing this morning, Natalie had submitted a full price bid for the house for her clients, confident that the seller would accept and the feather would be solidly in her hat. Less than an hour later, Max had called her back to let her know that Wes's clients had submitted a higher bid right after hers, and wanted to know if her buyers wanted to increase their offer. Thus, a bidding war had ensued, with back-and-forth phone calls all day long between her, her clients, and Max, who was representing the seller's best interest.

Her clients wanted the house, but it seemed that Wes's buyers wanted it more. For every offer she submitted on behalf of the Sandersons, his client outbid. The one-point-six-million listing was now up to one-point-seven hundred and fifty, which was Wes's buyer's last bid. Natalie was now anxiously awaiting a return call from the Sandersons to see if they were willing to go any higher.

She nearly jumped out of her chair and Richard chuckled when her phone vibrated and chimed on her desktop, and the name Jeff Sanderson showed up on the caller ID. Taking a few seconds to collect her composure and to send a silent plea up to the betting gods that her clients would come through for her, she answered in a calm, even voice . . . only to have all her hopes crushed when Jeff said, "My wife and I decided not to increase our bid. We're backing out."

All of Natalie's optimism plummeted in that moment, and the back of her throat grew dry from disappointment. She'd known that with every increase, they were getting further and further away from what the Sandersons could comfortably afford, but a part of her had been holding out hope that Wes's client would fold first.

Jeff told her that he'd like to look at other similar houses in their price range, and she was at least grateful that somewhere down the line was a million-dollar sale. But not one that would win a bet against Wes.

More painful was making the call to Max, to let him know that her client had backed out of the bidding—which was equivalent of her conceding defeat.

"You did well, Natalie," Max said, and she could hear in his voice that he felt bad that she'd lost the bidding war. "I'm sorry it didn't work out for your client."

"Thanks, Max," she replied, appreciating his kindness, instead of him saying something to kick her when she was down. He was a great guy, and she was truly bummed she wasn't going to get the opportunity to work with him at Premier Realty.

She disconnected the call and glanced up at Richard, who looked disappointed on her behalf. He knew how important this had been to her. It hadn't been just about winning a bet against Wes—though that would have been a nice cherry on top of the sundae—but more about proving that she had what it took to work for a luxury real estate firm. Specifically, Wes's firm.

"I was hoping to take you out for a celebratory drink, but I'm thinking this situation calls for drowning yourself in something rich and chocolatey at Ghirardelli's," Richard said like the good friend he was.

She managed a small smile, but before she could reply, her phone vibrated and chimed—but this time with a text message. From Wes. She'd expected him to gloat, but his note was short and concise.

Meet me at Navy Pier beneath the main arch at nine p.m. tonight.

She had no idea what he had planned, but she'd agreed to do whatever he asked, without complaint. She was beginning to regret giving him that kind of power over her, but she'd never reneged on a bet, and she wasn't about to start now.

WES HADN'T HEARD back from Natalie after sending his text, and with it nearly nine p.m., he was beginning to wonder if she was going to show. He'd been standing beneath the Navy Pier sign for the past ten minutes, and for a late August evening, it was thankfully cool instead of humid. But as each minute ticked by without any sign of his sexy adversary, he had more doubts about her meeting him as he'd requested.

Which wasn't like Natalie at all.

Even as a young kid, while she'd always been competitive, she'd never been a sore loser. No, failing at anything only made her more determined and driven to conquer whatever had eluded her grasp. He wasn't sure how she was going to spin this loss into something positive, and maybe she'd come to the same conclusion, as well, which would explain her possible no-show.

Five minutes after nine, just as he reached into his pocket for his cell phone to call Natalie, he caught sight of her approaching the pier. She was taking her own sweet time walking toward him, as if she hadn't kept him waiting. He knew her well enough to realize it was a deliberate slight on her part, that even though she'd obeyed his request, she was doing so on *her* terms. And Jesus Christ, that defiance of hers made his dick twitch at the thought of taming her in the bedroom, of making her give up control to him and enjoy doing so.

Yeah, nice fantasy, Sinclair.

Unlike the silk blouses she favored for her business attire during the day, tonight she was wearing a formfitting black tank top that molded to her full breasts and was tucked into a pair of black skinny jeans that looked just as tight. The neckline of her top scooped low enough to tease him with a glimpse of the soft upper swells of her breasts and the cleavage in between—which was probably her intent. Her unbound glossy hair shone in the overhead lamplight, and a few long silver necklaces accentuated her outfit and bounced against her breasts with each step she took toward him.

But it was the bright red strappy heels on her feet—the one pop of color against all the black—that piqued his imagination and prompted all sorts of filthy, dirty thoughts to take up residence in his head. Mainly, her wearing nothing but those shoes as she wrapped her legs tight around his waist while he fucked them both into oblivion.

He wiped that arousing vision from his mind just as she came to a stop in front of him. Oh, yeah, there was a rebellious spark in her gaze, and he was about to provoke her a bit more.

He crossed his arms over his chest. "You're late."

She lifted her shoulder in a casual, unapologetic shrug. "I couldn't find a parking spot."

At nine p.m. on a Wednesday night? He highly doubted that. He hadn't had an issue with parking, and that had been only fifteen minutes ago. "Make sure it doesn't happen again. Not without good reason."

"Yes, sir," she said, saluting him as if he were a sergeant, just to rile him in return. "What are we doing here, anyway? Are you planning on making me walk some kind of plank off the pier?"

He chuckled. "Nothing so dire, I promise."

Saying nothing more, he grabbed her hand in his and headed toward his destination, surprised when she didn't attempt to yank her arm back. He'd take that small concession, because a bigger one was coming up that would undoubtedly test her fortitude.

Even before he'd won the bet, he'd decided that this adventure would be their first battle of wills, and there was no doubt in his mind that she was going to do everything in her power to wheedle her way out of this challenge. But he wasn't backing down. Her acquiescence would set the tone for the next two weeks and would make her realize who was in charge.

Him.

They walked by restaurants, shops, and

some of the major attractions on the pier. When they passed the iconic Ferris wheel and it finally dawned on her where he was going and what they'd be doing, she stopped in her tracks, and with a hard pull, she extracted her hand from his. Expecting nothing less from Natalie considering what awaited her, he turned around and prepared himself for the fight.

"What the hell, Wes? We are not getting on that thing." She pointed an offending finger at the Centennial Wheel, which was like a luxurious, enclosed Ferris wheel that reached heights of over two hundred feet.

The high, aerial ride was like a throwback to their youth. It reminded him of a childhood incident, and the one and only time he'd ever seen Natalie give up on something she wanted so badly, and that was to join him and her brother in the tree house that her father had built in their backyard. At ten years old, she'd made it up the ladder only once, because one look down and she'd nearly hyperventilated. Her father had to climb up to rescue her and carried her down while she kept her eyes squeezed shut.

Wes and Connor couldn't have been happier that she never again attempted to scale the ladder, because it made the tree house the one place they knew for certain they could escape to without Connor's pesky younger sister tagging along and annoying them. It had been their hangout, boys only, and Natalie had hated that she couldn't join them.

"You'll be fine," he said with a persuasive smile. "I paid to have one of the VIP pods all to ourselves, so there will be plenty of room inside."

Her pretty blue eyes glared daggers at him. "Why are you doing this to me?"

"Because I've always wanted to go on this ride," he said, which was the truth. Partially. "Oh, and because you lost the bet and I'm asking you to."

She narrowed her gaze, which did nothing to conceal the apprehension etching her features. "You're such an asshole, Wes."

He laughed, not the least bit insulted. It wasn't the first time she'd called him a derogatory name, and he had a feeling it was her defense mechanism kicking in. "This is your chance to prove to me that you're going to uphold your end of the deal for the next two weeks, no matter what I ask."

Her chin lifted, that feisty, stubborn vixen

taking over. "If I throw up all over you, it's going to be your own damn fault."

"I'll risk it. It's all about mind over matter."

A huff of breath escaped her pursed lips, but before she could say anything more, he grabbed her hand once again and led her through the line to the modern-style Ferris wheel. Since he'd purchased VIP tickets, they were immediately ushered onto one of the gondolas, and seconds later, the glass doors closed after them, giving Natalie no time to protest or give in to her cold feet.

"Jesus," she said in a horrified voice as she sat down in one of the chairs and covered her eyes with her hands. "The floor is made out of glass!"

He looked down as the wheel moved upward to load the next cab, and sure enough, he was able to see everything below them. "Cool."

"It's not cool." Her words were muffled by the hands still masking her face. "It's terrifying."

He rolled his eyes at her overly embellished act. There was no way he was going to allow her to hide for the entire ride, which defeated the purpose of this outing. Gently grasping her wrists, he pried her hands away to reveal her apprehensive features as he pulled her to her feet. Her wide eyes latched onto his, and while he acknowledged her trepidation, he suddenly wanted her to actually enjoy this ride and the spectacular view of the city at night.

"Two rules, Natalie," he said softly as he led her to one of the windows with a metal bar for her to hold on to. "You remain standing for the entire twelve-minute ride, and you keep your eyes open, too."

"I know I already called you an asshole, but it bears repeating," she muttered as the gondola continued to climb higher and higher into the night sky. "This is cruel and unusual torture."

"I'm not trying to torture you." Okay, maybe he was, just a little bit. He liked having that advantage over her.

He curled her fingers around the metal bar so she had something to hold on to, and still standing behind her, he braced his own hands beside hers on the rail to give her a feeling of safety. Except the intimate position caused the front of his body to brush against the back of hers, and that's all it took for his cock to register the close proximity of her ass. With her wearing those hot-as-fuck heels, she was the perfect height for him to bend her forward and tunnel his shaft along her soft, wet pussy.

He felt her body tremble and heard a soft, strangled moan catch in her throat. The arousing sound was like a slow stroke to his hardening dick, which made him feel like the asshole she'd called him because he was fairly certain those noises coming from her were dismay and not a response to the sexual awareness he was dealing with.

She drew in a shaky breath as they reached the very top of the rotation, then groaned again as they began their slow descent down the other side. "This is so . . . damn . . .high."

"I won't let anything happen to you," he promised, and meant it. Despite daring her to get on the ride, he'd never do anything to deliberately hurt her.

"You can't stop the glass bottom of this stupid thing from falling out!" she snapped back.

Holding back his amused chuckle took effort. "Dramatic much?" he teased.

He felt her legs start to buckle, and he instinctively secured an arm around her waist—which brought her backside flush to his body. He caught a whiff of a soft, feminine scent—the one he'd always associated with her—and wondered if she realized that she'd somehow turned the tables on him. That *he* was now the one being tortured.

Her breathing grew rapid, and she suddenly turned around in his arms so she was facing him. Her eyes were huge, her pupils dilated with a surprising amount of fear he hadn't anticipated, and genuine angst was written all over her expression.

"I can't do this," she said, panting with anxiety, her complexion pale. "Oh, God, I'm going to pass out!"

He had an *oh, shit* moment as he realized she wasn't joking or exaggerating, and that *he* was responsible for her oncoming panic attack. Remorse immediately kicked in, and feeling like a jerk for pushing her further than she was comfortable, he released his hold on the steel bar and framed her face in his hands. He forced her to concentrate on him as she gasped for air, quickly on her way to hyperventilating. He knew heights weren't her favorite thing, but he truly had no idea the extent of her fears.

"Breathe, Natalie," he ordered firmly, knowing what it had cost her to give in when she was so strong-willed and had no doubt wanted to prove herself capable of handling the ride. "Just keep looking at me."

He continued to coach her on inhaling and exhaling and eventually felt her body relax. Her heaving chest calmed, and that hysterical look in her eyes gradually ebbed into something so soft and vulnerable it hit him square in his chest and stole *his* breath. His heart raced as they stared into each other's eyes, the ride no longer her focus as her anxiety diminished and awareness took its place.

Her lush mouth parted on a soft sigh, and the sight of her pink, wet tongue slowly gliding across her lush bottom lip was like an irresistible tease, fueling his need to taste her, to finally give in to the desire that kept him up late at night, imagining how she'd feel moving beneath his hard body and moaning his name as she came for him.

With his palms still cradling her face, Wes tipped her head back a few inches so that her mouth was poised beneath his, waiting for some kind of sign that she was opposed to what was about to happen between them. Instead, she whispered his name like a plea, destroying any last bit of restraint he'd been holding on to.

He doubted a single kiss would satisfy years of wanting Natalie, yet he couldn't stop what was about to happen, even knowing how wrong it was to take advantage of this moment. But kissing her felt inevitable and as necessary as his next breath, like something inside of him would die if he didn't have her, just this once.

He stared into her clear blue eyes, the trust and reciprocal need lingering in the depths slaying him. The need he understood. But the trust . . . that was something he didn't deserve.

"I'm sorry," he murmured huskily, unsure if he was apologizing for making her ride the Centennial Wheel or for finally giving in to the urge to kiss her.

But the second he lowered his head and his lips touched hers, his reasons for being contrite no longer mattered.

Chapter Six

AS WES SELFISHLY took what he wanted, what he suddenly desperately *needed*, he fully expected Natalie to come to her senses and jerk away from him, to end the kiss with an indignant comment that would remind him what a fucking bad idea this was—and that he had no business putting his lips anywhere on Natalie's body.

It's what she *should* have done, because he lacked the power to do it himself.

Instead, she placed her hands on his hips and leaned into him, flattening her breasts against his chest and making him wish she was completely naked so he could feel those gorgeous tits against his bare skin. Her mouth was so soft and yielding, her perfectly shaped lips molding to his as if they'd been designed solely for his pleasure. And when they parted and she made that cock-squeezing sound in the back of her throat, he was helpless to resist the invitation to deepen the kiss, to sweep his tongue inside and explore.

Jesus . . . how could a mouth that was so full of fire and sass taste as sweet as cotton candy? The question seeped through Wes's mind as he released his hold on her face and slid his hands into her thick, luxurious hair, gripped the strands in his fingers, and tilted her head to the side so that he could slant his mouth across hers in another slow, hot, tempting kiss that had her hands gripping him tighter and her hips moving provocatively against his rock-hard erection.

He shuddered and groaned and with all the friction the two of them generated whenever they were together and the years of sexual tension always simmering beneath the surface between them, he always imagined that kissing Natalie would be equivalent of being swept up into a tornado. Hard and fast, wildly intense, and reckless.

Oh, he definitely had the urge to pick up the pace, to unleash all the lust he was deliberately holding back, but this unhurried seduction was equally potent on a whole different level. This brief moment of indulgence was also all he'd allow himself to enjoy, because anything more with this woman was pure wishful thinking, or fantasizing, for numerous reasons.

One of them being her brother, Connor. Messing around with his best friend's little sister was like committing friendship suicide, not to mention putting a strain on their working relationship. Those pertinent thoughts prompted Connor's fierce, *I'm going to fucking kill you for touching my sister* expression to flash in Wes's mind, and it was just what he needed to put a damper on his cock's overly eager hopes for some kind of happy ending.

Wasn't going to happen. Not now. Not ever, with Natalie.

The depth of his regret and disappointment was startling.

He loosened his hold on her hair, and with one last pass of his tongue against hers, he ended the kiss and lifted his head. Her lashes fluttered back open, the dazed look in her eyes and the dreamy expression on her flushed face dissipating as she gradually remembered where she was and realized who she'd been kissing.

Her hands instantly dropped from his hips

when it dawned on her how intimately she'd been touching him . . . as well as rubbing up against him, not that he was going to point that out to her when she seemed so stunned and confused by her response to him.

She tipped her chin up, her gaze narrowed warily on his face. "Why did you do that?"

"You mean kiss you?" he asked, wanting to be sure that's what she was questioning.

She nodded. "Yes."

He opted for the simple, easy answer. "Because you were panicking and I was trying to distract you from the ride." He slid his hands into the front pockets of his jeans and gave her a playful grin. "Did it work?"

"Yes," she admitted, albeit reluctantly. "Just don't do it again."

Before he could say anything more—not that there was anything else to say—the ride came to an end. As soon as the doors slid open, Natalie darted around him and rushed off the gondola as if her sexy heels were on fire. He followed her onto the platform, came up beside her, and lightly grabbed her elbow to guide her back out to the main area of the pier.

"Where are you parked?" he asked, fairly certain that she was ready to call it a night. "I'll walk you to your car."

"You don't need to do that," she said, rejecting his offer. "I'll be fine."

"It wasn't optional, Natalie. Where are you parked?" he asked again, this time in a tone of voice that brooked no argument.

With a slight huff, she relented and gave him the section number, which was close to where he'd parked, as well. They walked to her vehicle in silence, and when her MINI Cooper came into sight, she disengaged her alarm and unlocked the car with her remote.

Wes opened the driver's-side door for her but stopped her before she could slide inside. She glanced up at him, that wariness back again, which he knew he deserved after tonight's stupid idea but he hated anyway.

Maybe what he was about to say would help them get back on track. "I just wanted to tell you that did great with the Magnolia listing today," he said, meaning every word. "Your offers were strong, and you handled the bidding really well. You're a good, solid Realtor."

Her gaze softened at his compliment, but he didn't miss the flash of disappointment in the depths of her eyes. "I'm a good Realtor . . . just not good enough to work for Premier Realty."

He inwardly winced, hating the harsh way that sounded, when his reasons for saying no to employing her at the firm were more complicated than that. Since her comment was merely a statement and didn't require a response from him, he let it go, since it was obviously a bone of contention between them.

"By the way, keep your Friday evening open," he told her, bringing up his next request for her services. "I'm going to need you for the night."

A feisty, defiant spark lit her gaze. "What if I already have plans?"

"With Richard?" he automatically asked, his tone more obnoxious than he'd intended.

The corner of her mouth twitched with a mirth he didn't understand, which she contradicted with a noncommittal shrug that made him a little crazy. "Maybe."

Wes's gut churned with acid. He was not a jealous man. He'd never cared if the women he'd casually dated were seeing other guys, so why did the thought of Natalie going out with Richard make him want to stake a claim on a woman who wasn't even his?

"Cancel them," he said, unable to deny that he liked that the bet gave him the power to have

Natalie all to himself. "Poker night this month is being held at my place, and I need a hostess to make some appetizers, get us our beers, and clean up after we're done."

She wrinkled her cute little nose in distaste. "Now that sounds like a fun evening," she said, her tone droll.

He chuckled. "It will be. For us guys, anyway. And I'll need you Sunday afternoon for a few hours, too."

"Dare I ask why?" she asked skeptically.

"I have a surprise birthday party to go to for a friend, and you're going to be my plus one." Whether Richard liked it or not.

✧   ✧   ✧

"CRAP!"

Forty minutes after shutting off her alarm the following morning, Natalie woke up with a start, realizing that she'd dozed off again and had overslept. With a rush of adrenaline surging through her veins, she jumped out of bed and stumbled toward the bathroom to make up for lost time.

After her restless night of tossing and turning and her lack of REM sleep, she was bleary-eyed, her head felt as though it had been stuffed with cotton, and she was undeniably grumpy.

And it was all Wes Sinclair's fault. Not because she'd lost the bet to him yesterday and not because he'd coerced her onto the Centennial Wheel. Both of those things she could have dealt with, and in the moment, she had. No, it was that unexpected, toe-curling kiss that he'd planted on her that kept replaying in her mind in lifelike detail whenever she'd closed her eyes that was responsible for her sleep deficiency.

Not to mention the pulsing ache between her thighs that he'd instigated with that kiss. God, she hadn't been so hot and bothered since way before she and Mitch had broken up, and after a few hours of trying to ignore that persistent arousal thrumming through her body, she'd finally reached into her nightstand drawer and let her battery-operated boyfriend—fondly named Liam, for her fantasy freebie, Liam Hemsworth—get her off. He never disappointed.

But as she'd slid the vibrator through her wet slit and closed her eyes to summon Liam's face, it was Wes's gorgeous features that she'd seen dipping between her spread legs and his hands gripping her inner thighs as he kept them pushed wide apart so he could slide his wicked mouth across her needy pussy. With his dark, hot eyes looking up at her, he'd flicked his tongue along her clit until she'd come on a long, hard, shuddering orgasm.

As a fantasy, Wes was quickly replacing Liam as her go-to guy. He was sex personified, with a body built for sin and a mouth made for pleasure, and good God, she wanted more of him, even knowing what a huge mistake it would be to give in to the lust burning between them . . . which was why she'd told him not to kiss her again. It had been pure self-preservation on her part, because she wasn't sure she'd be able to resist him, or where another kiss like that might lead.

Then again, the shameless part of her that was attracted to Wes was very curious to discover what might happen between them if she allowed his lips on hers again. The possibilities were endless . . .

Since she'd overslept, she didn't have time to wash, blow-dry, and style her hair, so she clipped it onto the top of her head and took a quick shower. Once she was done, she pulled her hair into a sleek ponytail, applied her makeup, and put on a navy blue dress with white trim. Twenty minutes later, she was out the door.

Since she'd spent her extra time that morning catching up on her sleep, she skipped her morning ritual at the Espresso Shot and requested her latte and a banana nut muffin to go, then headed to the office. Just as she sat down in her cubicle and placed her breakfast on her small desk, Richard showed up, looking very handsome in a gray suit with a light pink tie and a curious gleam in his eyes.

He leaned against the partition separating her little work area from the other employees. "So, how was your date with Mr. Big Shot last night?" he asked without any other pleasantries.

She picked up her latte and swiveled her chair to face him, knowing he was dying to hear all the juicy details. "It wasn't a date but more about him asserting his male dominance and making sure I knew who was in charge for the next two weeks."

"Asserting his male dominance, huh?" Amusement and intrigue deepened Richard's voice. "I like the way that sounds. What did he do? Something kinky, I hope."

She wished. Natalie appreciated Richard's levity in the situation, which was just what she needed to chase away the last of her grumpiness. "No, he took me on the Centennial Wheel knowing I have a thing about heights . . . and then he kissed me." After dropping that bombshell, she took a quick drink of her coffee.

A slow, knowing grin eased across his lips. "And judging by that flush on your pretty face, you liked it."

There was no sense denying the truth. Not to Richard, anyway. "Maybe. Just a little."

Richard crossed his arms over his chest and raised a brow that said, *You're such a liar.*

"Okay, I liked it a whole lot. But I also told him not to do it again," she said since she was being honest and baring all the finer points of the evening to him.

"Why the hell would you do that?" He stared at her as if she were insane for denying herself the pleasure of having Wes's mouth on hers again. "You *let* him kiss you, you admitted to enjoying it, so why are you sabotaging the chance to have a little naughty fun with a guy who clearly turns you on?"

She popped a piece of her banana nut muffin into her mouth and chewed for a few seconds, giving herself a bit more time to formulate that good ol' argument that always put her attraction to Wes in perspective. She swallowed, took a drink of her latte, and explained.

"I'm not trying to sabotage anything. I'm trying to be . . . smart." She set her paper cup on her desk and reclined in her chair. While everything that had happened with Mitch had messed with her head, and she was still trying to repair the damage to her heart, there were other factors to consider. "Wes is my brother's best friend. They work together, and if we started messing around and it ended badly, it would put a strain on their relationship. I don't want to be responsible for that. Besides, despite that kiss last night, Wes has always kept me strictly in the friend zone . . . or more recently, the frenemy zone," she said humorously.

Richard slid his hands into the front pockets of his trousers and tipped his head to the side. "First of all, who says your brother has to know that you're doing the dirty with his best friend? Clearly, if Wes is keeping you in the friend zone despite the fact that I saw him eye-fucking you yesterday morning at the coffee shop, then I'm betting he'd be down to having a discreet fling with you if you showed interest. It's a win-win situation."

"Are you *advocating* that I have an affair with

Wes?" And that's all it could ever be with a commitment-phobic guy like him. Just sex and pleasure . . . and no emotional involvement on any level. She wasn't in the market for another broken heart, and that's what Wes did best.

"If he batted for my team, I'd be all over that fine ass," he said, and Natalie laughed. "Seriously, though, you have two entire weeks of opportunity, so why not take advantage of it? Think of him as your rebound guy after Mitch. A hot, no-judgment palate cleanser of anything-goes sex before you get back into the dating game."

Natalie bit her bottom lip as certain body parts tingled at the thought of having anything-goes sex with Wes. She couldn't believe she was giving Richard's suggestion serious considera-tion, but his reasoning made sense. She hadn't been with a guy since her breakup with Mitch, and if she was honest with herself, Liam couldn't compete with the feel of a hot, hard man pumping his cock inside her or the deca-dent stroke of a tongue across her nipple, the sharp bite of his teeth in tender places . . .

Richard smirked at her as if he'd been privy to the arousing images filling her head. "You're thinking about it, aren't you?"

"It's an appealing idea," she admitted, and thought about the next time she was going to see him. "He wants me to be the hostess, a.k.a. a glorified maid, for his poker game with the guys on Friday night. I wouldn't mind getting even with him for making me go on that Ferris wheel last night, and get *him* a little hot and bothered in the process and see how it all plays out."

"Oh, I definitely have a few suggestions that will get a *rise* out of him," Richard said with a devious waggle of his brows, then shared his fun, sexy, outlandish ideas that would either make Wes want to throttle her or would change their relationship from frenemies to red-hot lovers.

She suddenly couldn't wait to find out which it would be.

Chapter Seven

WES WASN'T SURE what to expect as he opened the door for Natalie when she arrived Friday evening right on time at seven o'clock—a half an hour before the guys were scheduled to arrive for the poker game—but it certainly wasn't the tantalizing French maid costume she'd worn that immediately sparked a dozen dirty fantasies and instantly made his cock hard as granite beneath the fly of his jeans.

Ho-ly shit, was the only coherent thought he could form as he stared at the woman who was going to be the death of him. And his dick.

The classic black-and-white maid's dress was cut so damn low in the front that if he leaned a bit too close, he was certain he'd fall right into that soft V of cleavage, courtesy of some kind of amazing underwire bra that had her tits pushed up high, and a generous amount of pillowy softness showing above a white, lacy bodice. The outfit cinched tight along her torso, along with a frilly white apron, then flared into a short little skirt that ended mid-thigh, with layers of white ruffles peeking out from beneath. With a pair of black stiletto heels on her feet, her stunning legs looked endlessly long, and he couldn't stop imagining them draped over his shoulders or wrapped around his waist. Either scenario was hot as fuck.

"Are you going to let me in, or did you change your mind about needing me tonight?"

Amusement tinged Natalie's voice, and why not, considering his jaw had been literally hanging open in shock. He shut his mouth and lifted his gaze back to her face, not missing the daring glint in her brilliant blue eyes that told him she was going to make his life hell tonight. *He* was supposed to be the one in charge and calling the shots with this bet, but he should have known that this minx would put her own special twist on tonight's request to be a hostess at the poker game.

"No, I haven't changed my mind," he said, and opened the door wider for her to enter.

Somehow, someway, he'd deal with her fantasy-inducing costume. "Come in and I'll get you started on things in the kitchen."

She sashayed past him into his house with a satisfied grin on those pink, glossy lips he hadn't been able to stop thinking about since their kiss two nights ago. Knowing the layout of his place since she'd been there before, she headed in the direction he'd indicated. He followed her, watching the luxurious fall of her dark, wavy hair bounce against her back with every step she took.

"What do you want me to do first?" she asked when they arrived in the kitchen and she turned around to face him.

How about getting on your knees, parting those soft, fuckable lips and . . . Shit, shit, shit. Wes shut down that train of thought before it could fully form and forced his attention to the prep work he had waiting for her.

"You can put those bottles of beer in that steel tub and cover them with ice so they're cold when the guys get here," he said, pointing to the items he'd left on the counter, while trying not to let his gaze drop below her chin . . . and God, it was so fucking hard not to give in to that male instinct to take another peek at the lush swell of those breasts that were taunting him. "And I bought some appetizers that you'll need to put in the oven to heat up so they'll be ready about eight. Everything is in the freezer drawer at the bottom of the fridge."

"Okay." She walked to the refrigerator in those fuck-me heels, and with her legs deliberately locked straight, she bent at the waist to open the freezer drawer to retrieve the items.

He watched in fascination—God, he couldn't look away even if someone was holding a gun to his head—as the hem of her skirt rode up, flashing him with the creamiest expanse of thigh and black silky panties smoothed over the curve of her luscious ass. His shaft throbbed relentlessly, and swallowing the groan rising in his throat, he made a quick executive decision to save what was left of his rapidly dwindling sanity.

"You can't wear that outfit tonight," he blurted out.

She set the prepackaged appetizers on the counter, her eyes wide with a feigned innocence. "Why not?"

He braced his hands on his hips. "Your brother is going to flip his shit if he sees you in that risqué costume." Connor had always been protective of Natalie, even more so since that asshole ex of hers had cheated on her. This situation did *not* bode well for Wes at all. He could feel it in his gut.

"That's your problem. Not mine," she said without concern for his well-being when it came to her brother's displeasure.

She bent at the waist again as she looked through the bottom cupboards until she came across his baking sheets, and thank God she straightened before he could give in to the urge to run his palm over her perfectly toned ass she was waving like a red flag in front of a horny bull and maybe slide his fingers between her thighs and along the silky crotch of her panties while he was at it . . .

He exhaled sharply, which did nothing to subdue the agitation building inside him or ease the sexual frustration tightening around his balls like a vise. "How do you figure it's *my* problem?"

She turned his oven on to preheat, then opened a package of pizza rolls and dumped them onto one of the baking sheets. "You wanted a maid, so I'm going to look and act the part." She shrugged her shoulders, causing her breasts to jiggle enticingly.

His jaw clenched so hard it hurt as he watched her casually cut open a bag of frozen buffalo wings and arrange them on another tray. "I said a *hostess*, not a fucking French maid."

She glanced at him, a dark brow arching derisively over those bewitching blue eyes. "Yeah, well, considering what you want me to do tonight—cook, serve you guys, clean up your messes afterward—being a maid is a more apt description. Besides, I didn't bring anything else to wear."

He was desperate enough to get her out of that distracting costume to offer up his own clothing. "I'll give you one of my T-shirts and a pair of sweats."

She added the jalapeño poppers to the last baking sheet and tried to hide what looked suspiciously like a devious smile as she looked his way again. "Since this costume has a built-in bra, I'm not wearing one, and I don't want my breasts bouncing beneath a thin cotton T-shirt."

Neither did he, and especially not in front of Max, Kyle, and her brother. Jesus, she was killing him. Daring him, as if she knew he couldn't handle her traipsing around in that skimpy costume without thinking about all the filthy things he wanted to do to her while she wore the French maid dress.

He hated that she was winning this battle of wills, but since there was no changing her mind, or her outfit, he was forced to yield this round to her.

"Fine," he said, though he did have one concession to add. "Just please stop bending over in that costume because it flashes your ass."

The little tease batted her lashes at him. "I'll try not to."

She went to work putting the bottles of beer into the tub to fill with ice. Since Wes was done torturing himself, he went back downstairs to the basement that he'd turned into a man cave about a year ago, complete with a home theater system and a dedicated area set up for their monthly card game. He'd purchased a custom-made poker table with built-in chip racks and drink holders, and he started setting up for the game while listening to Natalie as she moved about in his kitchen upstairs.

At seven thirty the doorbell rang, letting him know that the three other guys had just arrived together via Uber, since there was no telling just how much alcohol might be consumed over the course of the evening. Wes bounded up the stairs to let them in, but his too-efficient hostess beat him to it. Good thing he'd told the guys that Natalie would be handling the refreshments and anything else they needed for the evening because of the bet. However, her outfit would undoubtedly cause an initial stir, and he prepared himself for the backlash.

She'd just opened the door as he came into view, enabling him to catch each man's response to Natalie's sexy ensemble. Max's eyes widened in surprise, Kyle gave her an appreciative once-over—the fucking asshole—and her brother, Connor, stared at his sister in confusion, which quickly evolved into disapproval.

Connor's brows snapped together in a frown as he addressed Natalie. "What the hell are you wearing?"

Her fingers played with the ruffled hem of her short dress in a self-conscious gesture no doubt designed to gain her brother's sympathy. "Wes requested a maid for tonight's game—"

"Not a maid. A *hostess*," he corrected, but the less derogatory term didn't seem to make any difference to Connor, who'd shifted that unsettling gaze on Wes that spoke a loud and clear *what the fuck, dude?*

"I've got your appetizers in the oven," Natalie said in a cheerful tone. "You guys head downstairs and get settled in, and I'll bring everyone an ice-cold beer."

She spun around, causing her flouncy skirt to swirl way too high and expose way too much thigh as she returned to the kitchen. Once again, Wes was privy to each man's response as they watched her retreat. Always the respectful gentleman, Max's features were amused. Kyle was intrigued, and Connor was now openly glaring at Wes as the trio walked inside the house.

"Are you fucking serious, Wes?" Connor said in a low, hissing voice as they all headed down to the basement. "I can't believe you made my sister wear that ridiculous costume. It's so short you can almost see her ass, and her boobs are falling out of that nearly nonexistent top."

Wes opened his mouth to issue a reply— mainly that the outfit hadn't been *his* idea or suggestion—but Connor wasn't done with his rant.

"I know she lost the bet and the two of you are constantly trying to one-up each other, but objectifying my sister like that is not cool, man."

Kyle snickered at the reprimand Connor

had just delivered, and Wes shot his instigating friend a dirty look. He thought about defending himself, but at this point, he was certain that Connor wouldn't believe him, anyway, if he told him that his sister was yanking his fucking chain or, rather, jerking his dick. It certainly felt that way.

So, he let it go, hoping that Connor would calm down after a beer, or two or three.

The poker table was set up for their regular game of Texas Hold 'em, and after everyone was settled in their seats, Wes dealt the first two cards. They all picked up their hand, checking what they had before tossing out their initial bet. He placed three more community cards face up on the table just as he heard Natalie coming down to the basement, along with Kyle's low, muttered *Jesus* that prompted Wes to glance up to see what had captivated his friend's attention.

Voluptuous tits and gorgeous legs, that's what had Kyle so enthralled. Max's and Connor's backs were to the stairs, and they were both studying their cards, but Wes and Kyle had a direct view of the temptress descending the stairs, carrying four longneck bottles of beer—two in each hand. It was like watching one of those slow-motion movie scenes as her long hair billowed around her shoulders and her breasts bounced in time to each careful step she took in those impractical high heels.

"*Damn*," Kyle said beneath his breath, prompting Connor to glance across the table at him to see why he'd cursed.

At least Kyle was smart enough to immediately look down at his cards, and it was a good thing, too, because Wes didn't want to have to gouge his friend's eyes out for ogling Natalie's finer assets. And when the hell did he become so possessive about a woman who wasn't even his? He was fairly certain the answer to that question was the moment he'd kissed her on the Centennial Wheel and she'd opened her warm, sweet mouth and kissed him right back . . . not as a friend but as a woman who was as hot and hungry for him as he was for her.

Yeah, that kiss had been a game changer, causing a definite shift in their attraction, and he couldn't deny that despite every reason he had to keep his mouth off of hers and his dick tucked away safely in his pants, it was getting more and more difficult to deny just how badly he wanted her.

As they placed another round of bets based

on the cards in their hand and on the table, he revealed another card while Natalie set a bottle of beer in each of their drink holders that were built into the table. As she rounded behind him, he realized what a fucking fantastic hand he held—five cards of the same suit—and anted up once again.

"Wow, it's quite hot in here," Natalie said as she passed by Wes again, pulling his head out of the game as she fanned herself with her hand. "In fact, I think I'm *flushed*. Anybody else feeling flushed?"

What the hell? Did she just give up his hand?

"I'm out," Max said as he put down his cards, the half grin on his face telling Wes that, yes, Natalie's comment had definitely influenced his decision to fold instead of tossing another bet into the increasing pot.

"Me, too," Connor chimed in, followed by Kyle.

Wes glanced at Natalie with a frown, and she gave him a guileless little shrug. No doubt about it, she'd just sabotaged his hand. When she did it a second time, making an odd remark about *straightening* his chips, the guys immediately knew what hand he was holding. Max and Kyle folded, but Connor upped the ante and won with a royal flush.

As he shuffled the deck, Wes gave Natalie a pointed look. "Don't you have appetizers to attend to or something?"

"Sure, I could go check on them."

He caught the mischievous gleam in her eyes before she started back up the stairs. He didn't even want to know what had prompted that look, but he was immediately suspicious. Once she was gone, he breathed a sigh of relief and dealt the next hand.

"I have to say, it's quite amusing so see a woman get the better of you," Max mused out loud as he picked up his cards.

"How so?" Wes asked, refusing to verbally admit that Natalie *was* in the process of outwitting him tonight with her clever pranks. First the French maid costume, then her comments that gave away his cards. What else did she have in store for him?

Max shrugged. "Just that women are usually falling at your feet or blinded by your charm, which makes them easy for you to influence."

"Or manipulate," Connor chimed in after taking a drink of his beer, seemingly still a little peeved over the risqué maid outfit.

"Yeah, that, too," Max agreed with a grin.

"Natalie, on the other hand, has no problem thumbing her nose at your rules and doesn't take your crap. She knows how to keep you on your toes and doesn't seem too worried about consequences."

Which was one of the many things that turned him on about her, that sassy defiance of hers, compared to the complacent, always-wanting-to-please-him women he was used to. "She *should* be worried," Wes grumbled, because his palm was suddenly itching to make contact with her ass. She certainly deserved a spanking for her bad behavior tonight.

Connor's gaze narrowed on Wes. "What's *that* supposed to mean?"

Wes sighed, cherishing his manhood way too much to reveal his dirty thoughts to his best friend about his own sister. "Nothing. It means nothing."

Connor didn't look convinced but let it go, and they played another couple rounds of poker without Natalie prancing around and distracting the hell out of Wes. It was quiet and calm and relaxing while they focused on their game, until about fifteen minutes later, when he caught a subtle whiff of something acrid.

"Something smells like it's burning," Kyle

said right then, confirming that Wes wasn't imagining things.

"Yeah, I smell it, too," Max said.

Wes glanced toward the stairs and could have sworn he saw a faint swirl of smoke coming through the doorway. He frowned. Something definitely wasn't right. He placed his cards facedown on the table and stood up to go and check things out just as the shrill sound of the fire alarm blared through the house.

"What the fuck?" Worried about Natalie, Wes bolted up the stairs with the other three guys tailing him and followed the trail of smoke into the kitchen, where it was the thickest and most pungent. "Natalie? Everything okay in here?"

"I'm fine," she assured him, nonplussed as she pulled the appetizers from the oven and set the scorched trays of food on the stove. Coughing a few times, she waved the potholder in the air to try and cut through the smoke, until the fire alarm finally went quiet again. "I think I left the appetizers in the oven longer than I was supposed to."

An understatement, Wes thought, his eyes stinging from the lingering haze in the kitchen. Everything was burnt to a crisp and inedible and looked as though she'd cooked it with a blow torch. Hell, maybe she had. Tonight he wouldn't put anything past her.

"Geez, Nat," her brother said, unable to disguise the disappointment that he wasn't going to get fed tonight. "It's not that difficult to heat up pizza rolls, wings, and jalapeño poppers."

She gave all four of them a contrite look that Wes didn't believe for a second. "I'm really sorry, guys. And this was all of the appetizers that Wes had."

Surprise, surprise, Wes thought sarcastically.

"What are we going to eat?" Kyle asked, a bit grumpily. "I didn't have dinner and I'm hungry."

"We'll have a couple of pizzas delivered from Dominos." Wes pinned Natalie with an *I know exactly what you're up to* kind of look, because he knew damn well she wasn't as incompetent as she was making herself out to be. "Think you can handle making the call?"

"Of course I can." The impudent minx rolled her eyes at him, as if *he* was the inept one. "You all go back to your poker game, and I'll order the pizzas and clean up this mess," she said, indicating the charred appetizers.

As the four of them headed back down to the basement, Wes's intuition told him not to trust Natalie, but how badly could someone screw up a pizza order?

Pretty fucking badly, he learned a half an hour later as she brought down the delivery boxes, set them on a side table with paper plates and napkins, and opened up the lids to reveal two of the grossest combinations of pizza toppings he could ever imagine.

She gasped and did a hell of a job rounding her eyes in shock as she looked at the pies. "Oh, my God, they totally got my order all wrong! I said pepperoni and *mushrooms*, not extra anchovies! And this one that has nothing but pineapple and jalapeños on it should have been a BBQ chicken supreme!"

Wes wanted to call bullshit so badly but managed to bite his tongue.

Kyle wrinkled his nose as he caught the strong scent of fish wafting in the air, since the ratio of pepperoni to anchovies was skewed toward the slimy-looking bait. "Okay, that's just disgusting."

"It's not that bad," she disagreed to the four men standing around the table, none of them wanting to be the first to sample the offensive pizzas. "Just pick off the anchovies the best you can, and you never know, pineapple and jalapeños might be an awesome combination."

"Oh, come on, Natalie," Connor groaned in frustration. "I get that you're screwing with Wes for making you be the maid tonight, but why do *we* have to suffer, too?"

"*Finally* someone else is catching on to her antics," Wes said, tossing his hands in the air.

"I have no idea what you're talking about." Natalie batted those long lashes at him and spun around to head toward the stairs. "I'll go get you all a round of cold beers to go with your pizza."

"Yeah, we're going to need it to wash down the nasty taste of anchovies," Kyle called after her.

All four of them remained where they were standing, staring at the pizza with varying degrees of apprehension, none of them eager to be the first to dive into this new culinary experience.

The loud, obnoxious grumble of Kyle's stomach forced the other man to make a decision. He swore beneath his breath, picked up a plate, and grabbed a slice of each pizza. The repulsive look on Kyle's face was comical but reflective of how all of them felt about the objectionable toppings they were about to consume.

They all sat back down at the table and began picking anchovies off their pizza, and even with them gone—at least what they could see of them—the salty, fishy taste was prominent in each bite. The jalapeño and pineapple combo was no better, and Wes was grateful for the ice-cold beer that Natalie delivered that helped cut through the heat and aftertaste lingering in his mouth. Ugh.

After finishing two slices, he told the guys he'd be right back and headed straight for the master bathroom and his toothbrush. He didn't even feel one bit guilty that he had the luxury of brushing his teeth and using minty Scope to rinse the despicable flavor out of his mouth, even though the other guys had to suffer.

He returned, and while Natalie cleaned up after their snack, they started another game. She picked up their paper plates—piled high with anchovies and some jalapeños—and tossed them into a trash bag. She went around the table, and when she arrived next to him, he felt the brush of her enticing chest against his arm—intentional, no doubt—as she reached for a crumpled napkin in front of him. He exhaled slowly and calmly and managed to ignore the physical taunt of her breasts, and just when she started to move away and he thought he could truly relax, her hand knocked his bottle of beer out of the holder. He watched with a sense of foreboding dread as the bottle tipped over completely, and the cold contents poured right into his lap.

The chilled liquid shocked his system, and he sucked in a sharp breath and shoved his chair away from the table, which did no good since the front of his jeans were already drenched through.

He lifted his narrowed gaze to Natalie. What. The. *Fuck*.

"Oh, damn," he heard Max say in a low voice that was edged with laughter.

"Yeah, the shit is about to get real," Kyle added.

"I'm so, so sorry!" Natalie exclaimed as she went to grab a napkin from the side table. "I can't believe how clumsy I am!"

Clumsy, my fucking ass. Natalie was one of the most agile, coordinated women he knew.

She returned quickly and started rubbing and pressing against the front of his jeans with

CARLY PHILLIPS & ERIKA WILDE

the thin napkin to soak up the beer, but it had already seeped through to his skin. He gritted his teeth as her fingers grazed along his rapidly hardening cock, and he couldn't deny that for a brief moment he let himself think about how her bare hand would feel wrapped around his shaft and stroking the length in her tight fist . . . until he came to his senses and realized they had an audience, and Connor would likely murder him for getting a boner when his sister *was just trying to help*.

He grabbed her wrist and yanked her hand away before the situation could get any worse. "Stop," he snapped, his frustration—mostly sexual—getting the best of him. "I'm waving the fucking white flag, okay?" It went against his grain to surrender, especially when he'd won the bet and *she* should have been way more cooperative this evening.

She bit back a smile, but he didn't miss the triumphant sparkle in her gaze. "Oh, okay," she said, somehow sounding naive, as if she had no idea the havoc she'd wreaked on him tonight.

She was a damn good actress on top of everything else.

Connor scowled at him. "That's what you get for making Natalie wear that ridiculous outfit and bossing her around."

Wes exhaled, slow and deep, to keep from responding to that false statement. He'd done neither but didn't bother defending himself when Connor had already pegged him as the bad guy. God, he was done with the poker game and the guys. But he was far from finished with Natalie.

"The game is over," he announced, and stood up, all too aware of the big wet spot on his jeans, but on the upside, at least his hard-on had subsided.

"Yeah, I figured as much," Kyle said, standing along with Max and Connor. "But it was definitely an entertaining evening."

Wes followed them up the stairs and to the door, while Natalie disappeared into the kitchen. Once the guys were gone, he closed and locked the door, then went to confront the woman who'd caused chaos with his poker night and his libido.

They had a few things to settle between them, and he had a feeling that a few more lines between them were about to be crossed.

Chapter Eight

WES STRODE INTO the kitchen, finding the counters and sink cleaner than he'd expected considering the appetizer fiasco earlier. In fact, Natalie was leaning casually against the counter, drinking water from a bottle, and looking very satisfied with herself.

Not for long.

She met his gaze, that gratification ebbing from her expression as she watched him walk straight toward her, his body language confident and back in charge. Awareness flashed in her eyes, and she licked her bottom lip a bit nervously now that they were completely alone, especially when he stopped in front of her, braced his hands on the counter on either side of her hips, and got right up into her personal space.

She set her water bottle aside but didn't try to back away—not that there was anywhere for her to go—but the sudden rise and fall of her chest gave away her body's reaction to him, to the years of combustible attraction they'd both suppressed up to this point. He had a feeling it was all going to boil over and burn them both.

He quirked an eyebrow at her. "Do you have something to say for yourself, Minx?"

Her big blue eyes went wide, though there wasn't an ounce of remorse in their depths for making tonight a complete disaster. "Umm, I'm sorry you had to cut the game short?"

She wasn't going to give an inch, but judging by his aching cock, he was more than prepared to give her a good seven of his own, depending on how this conversation played out. "Like you gave me a choice," he said sarcastically.

Her chin lifted a notch, but the heat in her gaze overrode any attempt she made at defiance. "I never said the guys had to leave or that the game was over."

Was she fucking serious? Yeah, she was, and he was about to set her straight. "Let me tell you *exactly* why I ended poker night early," he said, shifting his stance so that the rigid length of his erection made a distinct imprint on her bare thigh, since those crazy high heels she was wearing boosted her to his height.

"You're strutting around in this hot-as-fuck costume that has had my dick standing at full attention since the moment you walked into my place. You nearly burned my house down along with the appetizers. You ordered the most disgusting pizza I've ever tasted, and lastly, you were rubbing my goddamn cock with your hand less than ten minutes ago. Do you honestly believe I can think straight after *that*?"

The corner of her lips twitched with humor. "It's all about mind over matter, Wes," she said, repeating the words he'd used to get her onto the Centennial Wheel with him. As if it were that easy for him to shut off his dick's response to her.

God, that mouth of hers was so fucking sassy, and he was done tiptoeing around this chemistry between them and keeping his explicit thoughts about her to himself. And he was so done with her topping him from the bottom, trying to take control of any given situation just to prove she wasn't a weak, delicate female who would accede to a man.

Especially him.

"I'll give you mind over fucking matter," he growled. Finished playing nice when what he wanted was down and dirty, he slipped his hands beneath her short skirt so that his fingers were now gripping the soft, rounded curve of her bottom through her thin panties.

She gasped, her hands instinctively grabbing on to his biceps for support. The brazen move clearly shocked her, but she didn't protest his manhandling. In fact, the spark of desire illuminating her eyes and the tiny pulse beating erratically at the base of her throat told him that she liked the bit of rough play.

And he wasn't above testing that theory. "What I ought to do is bend you over and thoroughly spank your ass for undermining me and being so insubordinate tonight."

A pink flush spread across her cheeks, but the wanting in her gaze never wavered. "Maybe you should," she retorted huskily, recklessly.

Her words, her approval, were like a hungry jolt of lust straight to his already stiff cock. "Don't fucking tempt me."

She wet her bottom lip with her tongue, and the hands on his arms dropped to the hem of his T-shirt, then slid beneath until her fingers grazed that sensitive sweet spot right below his navel and right above the waistband of his jeans, tracing the lines of his abs.

"I *dare* you," she whispered, coming damn close to dwindling what little was left of his willpower to resist her.

"You're playing with fire," he warned in a low voice, wanting to make sure she realized exactly where all this teasing was heading.

"I know." Her lashes fell half-mast, and a challenging smile curved her lips. "I *double* dog dare you."

He had a brief flashback to their childhood and the many times *he'd* double dog dared *her*. It had been the ultimate taunt all those years ago, a sure way to get Natalie to do whatever he'd wanted because she'd never refuse any provocation. Now, she was turning the tables on him, and he didn't need any more incentive to give life to all the things he'd fantasized about doing to her for so fucking long.

But he wasn't opposed to making her suffer, just a bit more, for everything she'd put him through tonight. Payback was a bitch. And there was also the little matter of her telling him not to kiss her again that needed to be resolved before they went any further. Because kissing her was definitely going to happen, along with a whole lot of other wicked, illicit things that would guarantee she'd beg for more. And the thought of Natalie gasping and pleading and desperate for him had his blood running hot in his veins.

Releasing her ass, he lifted his hands to her face, holding her jaw in his grasp. He tipped her head back slightly, until her hazy eyes locked with his. Then he slowly, gradually lowered his mouth, so close to her parted, upturned lips that he could feel each of her impatient breaths against his skin as her anticipation grew. She was more than primed for him to seal the deal, but he held it just out of her reach.

Finally, she moaned in frustration. "What are you waiting for?"

He smiled at the exasperation in her voice. "I'm waiting for your permission to kiss you, since you were pretty adamant about not allowing me to do it again the other night." He dragged the pad of his thumb across her lower lip, marveling at his own restraint when he was dying to devour her. "I need to know it's okay, because I'm not going to stop at just one taste this time, and I can pretty much guarantee that once my lips touch yours, there will be no going back. My mouth is going to be all over this gorgeous, sexy body of yours . . . licking at your neck, sucking your tight, pert nipples, biting along your stomach, and if you're real good, I might even introduce your pussy to my tongue."

She shivered, even as her soft laugh rolled into a desperate, needy moan. "You have my permission to kiss me, and *please* do all those other things to me, too."

Ahhh, she's already begging, he thought with a grin. He loved her uninhibited response to him, her lack of modesty that gave him free reign with her body and her pleasure. And eventually, his, too.

His mouth finally descended on hers. Their first kiss had been a slow, easy exploration, a way to distract her from something frightening, but not this time. They were both in it for the sole purpose of physical enjoyment, and there was a whole lot of her he wanted to savor. He sank his fingers into her soft, luxurious hair, wrapped the strands around his fist, and angled her mouth beneath his for a hotter, deeper taste.

The kiss was a prolonged one by conscious choice, minutes longer than he normally spent on a woman's mouth. Lips interlocked and tongues tangled, moving in a sensual rhythm, easing in and out seductively, persuasively. Again and again. Natalie made a soft, purring sound in the back of her throat, which turned into a mewl of protest when he finally, reluctantly released her mouth from his . . . but only so he could nuzzle his face against her neck, trail his damp tongue up to her ear, and demand what he wanted next from her.

"Pull the top of your dress down so I can see and taste your gorgeous tits," he rasped, then lifted his head so he could see her face and watch this normally rebellious woman obey his order.

Her lips were wet and swollen, her eyes dark and aroused as they looked into his. She raised her hands to the elastic neckline of her French maid costume, slid the short sleeves a quarter of the way down both arms, then pulled the stretchy material over her full breasts, revealing those twin beauties to his avid gaze. He filled both palms with the soft, supple flesh, kneading them until they were firm in his hands, then rolled her tight nipples between his thumb and forefinger.

Her breathing escalated, and she shamelessly

pushed and rubbed her breasts against his hands, silently asking for more. His mouth was more than happy to oblige, and he dipped down, drawing first one taut crest, then the other between his lips, giving them equal treatment. He sucked them so hard and deep she moaned and gripped his hair, not to push him away but to pull him closer, to force him to take more of her, as much as his mouth could handle.

He scraped his teeth across each sensitive tip, knowing by the shudder that shook her body and the restless shifting of her legs that the sharp twinge had spiraled straight down to her pussy. He soothed her sore nipples with his tongue, leisurely licking each aching bud and reveling in the soft cry of need that made his cock throb and had him sliding a hand between her thighs and along the slick silk fabric of her panties that were soaked all the way through.

"*Wes.*" She breathed his name like a prayer, her hips moving against his stroking fingers, seeking a deeper penetration, a firmer friction.

He wanted her naked. Wanted to see her curves, feel her quiver beneath his mouth and hands, and taste every inch of her skin. Reaching behind her, he tugged the zipper of her dress down, and when the material fell to her hips, he didn't waste time shoving the outfit all the way down and off. He nearly tore off his shirt as she kicked the dress away, leaving her in just her panties, those sky-high stilettos, and the silky cascade of her wavy hair tumbling over her shoulders.

Jesus, she was stunning. Gorgeous and sexy and finally his to take.

Biting her lower lip, she skimmed her fingertips lightly down the center of his bare chest, tracing the rigid groove of muscles bisecting his abs. He gave her a moment to look and touch, to sate her own curiosity about his body, the only opportunity he'd allow before he took total control. He groaned when her palm brazenly cupped his solid erection through his still-damp jeans, when her fingers squeezed him in sheer torture as she unabashedly determined his size and shape more thoroughly than the last time she'd felt him up after spilling beer in his lap.

She was nearly naked in front of him, and she wasn't the least bit shy in her nudity, but confident and self-assured, and it was such a huge turn-on to be able to look his fill of her without any self-conscious issues getting in the way. Her generous breasts were perfectly shaped and tipped with pink nipples still hard and tight from him sucking them. While she continued to stroke his denim-clad shaft, he settled his hands around her rib cage and skimmed his thumbs beneath the swells of her breasts, loving the soft intake of her breath and the tantalizing shimmy-shake of her tits as she shivered from his caress.

He traced the indentation of her waist with his fingers, followed the flare of her rounded hips that were built to withstand a hard, pounding fuck, and trailed around to the soft globes of her ass that were made to cushion a man's driving thrusts. Hooking his thumbs into the waistband of her panties, he slid them down a few inches and leaned in close so his chest brushed against her nipples and his lips were near her ear.

"Is your pussy ready to get well acquainted with my tongue, baby?"

She turned her head slightly so she could whisper right back into his ear. "Yes, I do believe she's *very* ready. Shall I formally introduce the two of you?" Her voice was a husky, playful tease.

He chuckled. Nope, no timid reserve or sexual hang-ups with this girl, which made the thought of going down on her that much more appealing. "I think I can manage the introductions myself."

Shoving her underwear down her thighs, he impatiently followed the flimsy fabric's descent toward the floor, dropping to his knees in front of her so his tongue could properly greet her pussy. She braced her hands against the counter as he helped her step out of her panties, then he picked up one long, slender leg and draped it over his wide shoulder, giving him a fucking fantastic view of the pouty lips of her sex, spread open to expose her clit and dripping wet with her arousal.

Ignoring the relentless throb of his dick, he gently bit his way up the inside of her right thigh, nipping at her flesh and making her entire body twitch. He reached the heart of her femininity and tipped his head back to grin up at her. "I think your pussy is very excited to see me."

"Kiss her hello," she urged him oh-so-sweetly. "She likes kisses."

He smirked. "Does she now?" Who would have thought his first encounter with Natalie—the woman who'd become his frenemy—would be so filled with humor. And heat. Lots and lots of heat. It was a fucking heady combination.

She nodded jerkily, her fingers tightening on the edge of the counter as he dipped his head and blew a warm stream of air across her pretty, sensitive flesh. "And licking, petting, and stroking," she said on a rush of breath.

"Does she like to be fingered while she's being kissed?" he asked, dragging two fingers through her drenched slit and pressing the tips to her snug opening.

Natalie instinctively tilted her hips, angling for a deeper penetration of his fingers, which he wasn't ready to allow. "She's pretty much a hussy when it comes to oral sex. She likes it all."

He let a wicked smile curve his lips. "The dirtier, the better?"

The slow slide of his thumb along her clit made her moan. "I'm sure she could be persuaded to try anything once."

Oh, fuck me. That was like giving him carte blanche with her gorgeous body and allowing him free rein with all those filthy fantasies he'd been collecting over the years.

She was breathing anxiously, the needy look in her glazed eyes making him even hungrier to taste her, to give her the pleasure she so desperately wanted. With his gaze locked on hers and his hands gripping her thighs, he leaned in those last few inches and pressed his open mouth between her legs and slowly, leisurely licked his way to her clit. When he pumped two fingers into her tight body, her head fell back as her legs shook, buckled, and threatened to give out on her. She grabbed a fistful of his hair to steady herself, then, realizing the leverage it gave her, she rocked her hips against his mouth, chasing the suctioning swirl of his tongue all the way to a screaming, moaning, trembling orgasm.

Wes didn't stop there. He could have and normally did move things along so that his dick got in on the action and he could switch his focus over to his own mindless release. But he honestly couldn't remember the last time, if ever, that he'd wanted a woman with this much desire, where drawing every last ounce of pleasure from her became his main priority. Never had he spent so much time on his knees going down on a woman and eating her out because he enjoyed it, making her come more than once because he loved the way Natalie tasted, the way she cried out his name and clutched his hair to press his mouth harder against her pussy as she convulsed with a second climax that had her thrashing as though she'd been jolted with a live wire.

Wes pushed to his feet, wrapping an arm around Natalie's waist to make sure her legs didn't give out on her, while his other hand delved into her hair as his lips crashed onto hers in a deep, carnal, sexually charged kiss that was insanely hot. Infinitely deep. When he finally pulled his mouth from hers, she looked flushed and dazed, and for a moment he worried he'd gone too far, too fast.

Gently releasing her hair, he cupped the side of her face in his hand, using his thumb to tip her head back a bit more so she was looking into his eyes. "Are you okay?" he rasped, wanting to make sure they were still on the same page, that she was aware of where this was headed next. They weren't going to cross that line without her consent.

She nodded, a soft smile on her lips. "Yes, I'm better than okay."

"Good. Because I'm not done with you yet." Oddly relieved by her answer, he slid the hand that was around her waist down to her bare ass, stroking the silky-smooth flesh beneath his palm. He was already anticipating following through on the *double dog dare* she'd issued for him to spank her. "And after tonight's debacle, once we take this into the bedroom, I want you to prove just how obedient you can actually be."

Curiosity glimmered in his gaze. "You like your women submissive?"

Before tonight, he'd always dated women who were easy to handle, who didn't push his buttons and catered to whatever he wanted and needed, *when* he wanted or needed it. It kept affairs and flings simple and uncomplicated, and it kept his emotions out of the equation, which was what mattered the most.

But he couldn't deny that Natalie's spirit and fire turned him on. That she didn't make it easy on him. That she made him work for it and always kept him guessing. Yes, she pushed his buttons, and she'd never be one of those women who tried to do and say all the perceived right things to sway him into a committed relationship. She wasn't needy or clingy, and *submissive* was a word he'd never use to describe her.

"I like my women *accommodating*," he said instead, for the sake of their discussion and what he intended to do to her. "Tell me, Minx, are you willing to show me how contrite you are for being such a bad girl tonight?"

"Yes," she said without hesitating.

He didn't miss the glimmer of anticipation in her eyes, instead of the defiance he was used to encountering with her. Apparently, when it came to sex, she didn't mind participating in a little role playing and had no issues giving him the control.

God, could she be any more perfect? At the moment, he didn't think so.

He stepped back, offered her his hand, and inclined his head. "Then let's move this to the bedroom, where we'll both be more comfortable."

Chapter Nine

NATALIE PLACED HER hand in Wes's and let him lead her to his master bedroom down the hall, a part of her marveling at the fact that she was completely naked—except for the heels he didn't seem to want her to take off—while to her disappointment he still wore his jeans. But he had a beautiful back ... wide shoulders and toned muscles that sloped down his spine. She could easily imagine gripping that firm flesh while he drove deep inside of her and marking him with her nails.

Crazily enough, her softened sex pulsed at the thought, even though he'd already given her two phenomenal orgasms that should have more than satisfied her. But now that Natalie knew how good it felt to have Wes's mouth between her legs and his tongue doing the most delightfully wicked things to her girly bits, the greedy hussy wanted more. She wanted every dirty, indecent thing that Wes was willing to give her.

God, when had she become so wanton? She'd never been this uninhibited and shameless with Mitch. But then again, he'd never spontaneously gone down on her in the kitchen before like Wes just had, pleasuring her as if that was his sole reason for being on his knees—to worship her body, her pussy, and get off on watching her come not once but two freakin' amazing times.

No, Mitch had never been that adventurous when it came to sex, and she'd accepted their vanilla, lights-off, missionary style of fucking because sex wasn't everything in a relationship, right? What had been important was that they'd had the same goals for the future—marriage, having a family, creating the kind of life together that her parents had. Or so she'd thought. But maybe his ideals had shifted to include a woman other than Natalie because she'd been so focused on her job, her career, and hadn't seen the signs of Mitch's gradual withdrawal from their relationship.

And once Mitch had left her, Natalie had shut down her desires, which hadn't been difficult to do at the time. Other than the occasional romp with Liam for a quick orgasm, there had been no other men in her life. Until now. She was about to end her long dry spell with the one guy she'd fantasized about for years but never thought she'd ever bone—her brother's best friend and her nemesis.

Despite their attraction, she'd always known that Wes was a player and certified heartbreaker, which was the exact opposite of what she wanted in a guy, especially after being cheated on by Mitch. Then again, it wasn't as though Wes was asking for a lifetime commitment. Just hot, toe-curling, spine-tingling sex. As Richard had said, this was all about a convenient fling before she thought seriously about dating again. Wes was her transition guy, and she knew better than to have any expectations beyond sex.

Wes came to a stop at the foot of his huge king-sized bed. Facing her, he gently brushed her hair away from her cheek with his fingers, his gaze studying her features too intently. "You look awfully serious all of a sudden," he said, more intuitively than she would have given him credit for. "What are you thinking, beautiful?"

The genuine concern in his tone and his tender touch startled her. Ever since they were kids, they'd always been so competitive, so intent on provoking one another past the point of irritation. Even as adults, that same push-pull behavior had held true, but the fact that he'd sensed her deeper, more troubling thoughts enough to make sure she was okay shed light on him as more than just her business rival. *This* man's caring side that he rarely showed anyone was dangerous to her suddenly wildly beating heart.

All she knew in that moment was that she didn't want to think about Mitch anymore or her own shortcomings in the relationship that had caused him to stray, to make her feel less of a woman who hadn't been able to meet his needs. Not when she had a smokin'-hot guy standing right in front of her, more than willing and very capable of making her forget everything but sheer physical bliss.

She reached out and tucked her fingers into the waistband of his jeans, giving them a playful little tug. "I'm thinking I want your pants off so you're just as naked as I am."

A slow, sinful grin kicked up the corner of his mouth, and if Natalie had still been wearing panties, they would have hit the floor all on their own. "That I can do," he said, and had them stripped off, along with the rest of his clothing, in less than a minute flat.

She glanced down his body, taking her time to peruse all his masculine perfection. When she reached his straining erection, her pussy clenched instinctively. Appreciatively. If she'd thought he'd felt huge in her hand just a while ago, without the confinement of denim, he was inches longer and twice as thick.

She reached out and wrapped her fingers around his shaft and stroked him in her fist. His skin was hot, his cock hard and smooth against her palm. He pulsed and flexed in her hand, and when a bead of pre-come leaked from the tip, she brushed her thumb over the slit, smearing the silky fluid all over the plump head.

"*Fuck*," he rasped, and grabbed her wrist to pull her hand away, his chest heaving, his eyes smoldering. "That feels too damn good, but I *prefer* to be buried balls deep inside of your tight pussy when I come."

God, this man's filthy words were like a slow, heated caress right between her legs. Just as potent as his tongue had been against her clit. "I'd prefer that, too."

"Good to know we're on the same page." He nudged her a few steps backwards, until her knees hit the edge of the mattress and she toppled onto the bed. She came up on her elbows, watching as he strolled to the nightstand, retrieved a condom, and sheathed his cock. When he returned to the foot of the bed again, he met her gaze, his dark and tempting as he stroked his own cock in his hand.

His eyes traveled from her breasts all the way down to where her legs were slightly parted, giving him a teasing glimpse of her pussy. "You ready to show me how contrite you are for your naughty behavior tonight?"

She nodded, unable to deny how eager she was to comply with his demands, knowing the end result would mean more pleasure for her. "Yes."

He stood a few feet away, and despite not wearing a stitch of clothing, he still managed to exude a commanding, authoritative presence. "I want you facedown on the bed on your knees, with your chest pressing against the mattress and your arms extended straight above your head. I want your ass as high in the air as you can get it, but keep your legs pressed together."

She blinked at him in surprise, though

something dark, arousing, and forbidden swirled in her belly at the thought of assuming such a porn star position. She'd never done anything so brazen, so indecent, but she should have known that there wasn't anything about Wes that was vanilla when it came to sex.

When she took too long to contemplate his request, he inclined his head and smirked. "Did you misunderstand me?"

She quickly shook her head. "Umm, no." She'd heard him just fine.

"Then do as I ask, *now*, unless you want to increase your punishment?"

He seemed so stern, so assertive, and that show of dominance aroused her more than she'd ever thought possible, she realized, as she rolled onto her hands and knees and assumed the explicit position he was not-so-patiently waiting for. She stretched her arms above her head and kept her legs locked together as she raised her bottom as high as it could go, wondering how she could be such a strong, confident, self-assured woman in her daily life yet so willing to acquiesce to this man's orders in the bedroom.

But the answer didn't really matter, not when her body was already buzzing with anticipation, quivering with need.

With her cheek pressed to the soft, cool comforter and her back arched to accommodate her upturned hips, she closed her eyes as she felt Wes move onto the bed. He knelt behind her, pressing his knees against the outside of hers, pinning them together and preventing her from opening her legs at any time.

"Jesus, you have such a fine, pretty ass," he murmured as he kneaded the soft flesh in his hands. "It's going to look even prettier after I spank it. Are you ready to be disciplined for your actions tonight?"

Arousal and the slightest trickle of apprehension mingled inside her. "Yes," she whispered, and braced herself for the unknown.

"This is for tempting me with that French maid costume," he said, his voice low and rough as he spanked her right cheek.

She jerked in shock and moaned into the comforter, and he soothed the sting with a gentle caress of his palm, which was an unexpected and pleasant contrast to the smack he'd just delivered.

"This one is for giving away several of my poker hands." Another searing slap landed on her backside, causing her hips to buck against his and his erection to push insistently between her thighs.

The heavy pressure of his cock trying to work its way toward her pussy made her desperate to spread her legs, to coax his shaft to fill her up where she was starting to ache so badly she was tempted to put her fingers on her clit and ease the building tension all on her own. But there was no way to move her knees apart since he kept them restrained with his own, and she knew that he'd add to the punishment if she defied him by touching herself.

"And let's not forget the appetizers you deliberately burned and those disgusting pizzas you ordered." Two blows in quick succession had her gasping from the heat expanding like wildfire across her ass.

She grabbed at the comforter with her hands and whimpered, even as the initial pain ebbed into a tingling sensation that made her sex swell with need and slick moisture coat the insides of her thighs. God, how could she be so turned on by a spanking? Why was something that should have been degrading making her so frantic for yet another release?

"And finally, for spilling the beer in my lap." A crack of sound rent the air, making Natalie dizzy and breathless, her entire being trembling as her pussy grew softer, wetter, hotter.

A guttural groan echoed from behind her as Wes gripped her hips in his hands. "Seeing my handprint on your ass is so fucking hot."

The possessive tone of his voice did something to Natalie deep inside. Made her feel ridiculously desired and inexplicably vulnerable because of how badly she wanted him. As if feeling him moving inside her was as imperative as her next breath.

"Wes . . . I need . . ." God, she couldn't even explain in words what he did to her.

"I know what you need, baby," he murmured, suddenly sounding just as impatient as she was. *Finally.*

Still keeping her legs tight together, he guided his erection down the crease of her ass, gradually pressing that thick column of flesh deeper, farther, until the tip of his cock rubbed along the slippery cleft between her legs. He pumped his hips a few times, lubricating the length of his shaft with her arousal, then positioned himself at the opening that led to her core.

She could hear his erratic breathing behind her. So slowly, *so excruciatingly slowly*, he sank into her, forcing her to feel every single sensation of his erection rubbing against her inner walls, until he was as deep as he could go and she was stretched deliciously full.

It tore a moan of pleasure from her throat that merged with his equally strangled groan. He managed to reach up and grab a pillow and shoved it beneath her stomach, then pressed her hips down toward the mattress while keeping their bodies joined. The firm pillow kept her ass raised at just the right height and angle for Wes as he stretched out over her. He covered her from behind, his hard body surrounding hers, keeping her confined beneath him, to fuck as he pleased.

He pushed her hair off to one side, and bracing his forearms on either side of her, he nuzzled his face against the side of her neck as he withdrew to the head of his cock and lazily slid right back in again, groaning as her body clasped his dick in the softest, silkiest heat.

"I honestly thought this was going to be a hard, fast fuck," he rasped into her ear as he flexed his hips tight against her ass, completely fusing them together. "And maybe we'll work up to that, but right now, I want to feel *everything*."

Oh, Lord, so did she. "Yes . . ."

"This"—he pumped into her again, shuddering as he rolled his pelvis and she swallowed his cock whole—"is goddamn perfection. The way your tight, hot pussy is gripping me like a closed fist, the soft cushion of your ass buffering my thrusts . . . the way you're trying to spread your legs so you can take control. Not gonna happen until I let it, baby."

She whimpered, because everything about what he was doing to her was pure, delightful, sublime agony. He continued to torture her with his explicit words that made her internal muscles constrict around his cock. With the steady downward pressure of his body behind hers and the hand he slid beneath her hips and between her thighs so that the stroke of his fingers could add another level of need.

It was all too much . . . and not nearly enough. She was excruciatingly aroused, and she curled her fingers tighter into the bed covers, an anchor to hold on to and her only way to push back against each leisurely slide of his shaft, to entice him to take her harder, faster.

He chuckled at her efforts, the sound husky and full of sin. "Such a greedy girl. You want to fuck my cock?"

More than her next breath. "Yes . . . yes, *please.*"

The weight of his body behind her and on top of her eased up, enabling Natalie to finally rock her hips back against his, slamming his cock so deep inside her that she gasped at the intensity of it. She moved forward as much as Wes would allow, then back again, sliding up and down his shaft in an erratic rhythm while he worked her clit with his fingers.

His mouth touched down between her shoulder blades, trailing up to her neck for a rough love bite that made her buck beneath him. With a soft mewling sound of frustration, she pressed her ass up against his belly even higher, desperate for more friction to get her off.

"Push back against me, baby," he growled, clearly closing in on his own climax. "Harder. Faster. Grind your ass against my aching dick. Buck against me, take what you want. What you fucking need."

She did all those things, arching her neck and crying out as Wes lunged forward, plowing into her with a force that made her see a thousand bright stars. His next driving thrust, along with the way he applied exquisite pressure to her clit between two fingers, made her completely detonate. She cried out and clawed at the bed as her legs shook uncontrollably and her pussy milked his cock.

Only then did she feel Wes let go of his restraint. He pounded into her harder—fast and furious strokes that quickly turned short and erratic, as did his breathing. With one last jarring, feverish thrust, he stiffened against her ass, his harsh curse turning into a ragged shout of pleasure as he gave himself over to his own raging orgasm.

Chapter Ten

O NCE WES RECOVERED, he moved off of
Natalie and flopped onto the bed beside
her on his back. She felt boneless and couldn't
move her limbs, either, but she turned her head
and felt herself smile when he opened just one
eye to peek at her, looking adorably sheepish, an
amusing contradiction to the aggressive man
who'd all but fucked her brains out just moments ago.

They were both totally naked, lying on their
backs, staring at one another. His dark hair was
a gorgeous mess around his head, and the barest
hint of stubble was appearing on his jaw, and
she had to resist the urge to touch it with her
fingers, just to feel the coarse texture so she
could imagine later what it might feel like

abrading her skin in sensitive places.

It really wasn't fair that he could look so damn sexy when she was fairly certain she looked completely and totally debauched—by him. In fact, normally she'd be dragging a sheet over her body, but there was no sense feeling self-conscious about her nudity, not when he'd seen and touched just about every part of her, all in one night.

"You okay?" she asked with a soft laugh. Because, yeah, he looked totally wasted, and she couldn't help but feel a little ego boost that *she'd* done that to him.

"I'm great." He grinned back at her, and with a groan, he started to move off the bed. "But I'll be better once I get rid of this condom, so give me a sec. And while I'm gone, don't you dare move or cover that perfect body of yours."

She blushed at the compliment and remained right where she was while he padded off to the bathroom. He returned a few minutes later, crawling his way back up toward her from the foot of the bed until he was back by her side.

He looked momentarily disappointed. "Damn, I was hoping you wouldn't listen to my request so I could turn you over and spank you again."

She groaned at the memory of how hot his hand had felt smacking her tender backside. "I think I'm going to be a little sore tomorrow."

"I hope so," he said, a tad bit arrogant as he propped himself up on his side so he was looking down at her. "For two reasons. Because one, you were a very bad girl tonight and deserved a sexy punishment to remind you just who won our bet and who's in charge, which would be me, of course. And two, I want you to think of me every time you move or sit down and feel your panties chafing against your delicate, sensitive skin."

Of course he would, she thought with a mental eye roll. "I'm going to wear my best silk underwear so there will be no chafing involved."

A smirk tugged at his lips. "If I had my way, I wouldn't let you wear any panties at all for the duration of our bet," he said in a low, husky growl.

Her stomach did a little somersault as she shook her head. "I am *not* going commando, no matter what you say."

"We'll see," he murmured as he leisurely checked her out, from her face, down her naked body to her legs, and back up again. Then, he followed that up with his fingers, skimming them along the lower swells of her breasts and lightly trailing the tips down her sternum.

"What are you doing?" she asked, because he suddenly seemed so preoccupied, beyond the obvious.

He half grinned at her, and she tried not to let her heart flutter like an infatuated school-girl's. "I'm just confirming that you're not a fantasy." Those long fingers returned to her breasts and circled her nipples, and he watched as they tightened into hard, tight peaks. "That you're really in my bed and what we just did wasn't a figment of my imagination."

She raised a brow curiously at his revealing words. "Are you saying you've fantasized about me?"

"Too many times to count," he admitted with a sigh. "Though what we just did far surpassed any fantasy I've ever had."

His confession was so unexpected, especially when she thought of how many years she'd fantasized about *him.* The only exception to those lustful thoughts had been during her time with Mitch, when she'd packed them away, believing that he'd be the only man in her life for the rest of their days together.

But now she was single again, and she couldn't deny that Wes was the best sex she'd ever had. And like the greedy girl he'd called her, she wanted more. More hot, erotic encounters. More fantasies to explore. More of Wes being in control sexually and her enjoying *letting* a man take the lead because she knew it was all part of the game.

She'd never been a woman who slept around with numerous men, and she didn't want to start now. But as Wes bent down and licked her taut nipple before sucking it deep into his mouth and her body started purring with pleasure all over again, she couldn't deny that this arrangement of theirs could possibly benefit them both.

His teeth gently sank into the soft flesh of her breast, and she gasped and threaded her fingers through his hair, gripping the strands tightly to try and keep her thoughts grounded. "I . . . I think we ought to make an amendment to the bet," she said breathlessly, before she lost her nerve.

"Yeah?" His tone was mildly curious as his free hand cupped her other breast, squeezing the flesh and plucking her nipple with his fingers. "What do you have in mind?"

God, it was difficult to think straight while in the throes of being ravished by Wes, but somehow she managed to gather her words together. "Adding sex to the agreement, for the duration of me fulfilling my end of the deal."

"Why, little Natalie Prescott," he said, lifting his head from her chest so that she could see his dark, mesmerizing blue eyes rounded with feigned shock. "Are you propositioning me?"

She glared at him. He had no business looking scandalized, even if it was all an act, when he was probably a pro at propositioning women. "Yes, I am," she said, deciding to own it. "The way I see it, we can either go back to being frenemies and irritating each other while ignoring the sexual tension that has now been let out of the bag, so to speak, or we can take advantage of our situation for the next couple of weeks and enjoy more of this," she finished, waving an awkward hand between their naked bodies. Geez, she was so inept at this sort of thing.

The faintest hint of amusement touched his features. "So, you want to be fuck buddies?"

She inwardly cringed at the crass term, but hey, they might as well call a spade a spade.

"Fuck buddies, a hook-up, frenemies with benefits, a booty call, boning each other. Take your pick, as long as we're exclusive for the rest of the two weeks." That was a deal breaker for her, even if they were only having a temporary fling.

Quiet humor danced in his eyes. "Did you just say 'boning each other'?"

She shrugged and bit back a grin of her own. "Boning . . . forking . . . "

"Spooning?" he asked hopefully.

Never would she have imagined that Wes was a spooner. But she wasn't opposed to having his big, hard body tucked up behind hers every now and then. "That's negotiable."

He laughed deeply, and she realized that this was the first time they'd ever been so relaxed and at ease with one another. Who would have thought having dirty, x-rated sex would make them more civil to each other, that they'd be able to chat in bed naked and not want to throttle the other person? But that underlying tension seemed to have abated for now, and it honestly felt good to just *be* together without having her guard up around Wes.

He flattened his palm on her belly, his big hand and long fingers nearly spanning her hip to hip. A small frown marred his brows as he met her gaze. "How do you think your brother would feel about us 'boning'?"

His tone was light, his choice of word a tease, but she knew he wasn't joking around about the *brother* part of his question. He seemed genuinely concerned, which she found odd.

"We've already had sex, Wes, so that's kind of beside the point, don't you think? Besides, I'm an adult, and Connor doesn't have a say in who I sleep with, nor does he ever have to know. This ... you ... us ... we're both scratching an itch," she said, trying to find a way to keep everything breezy and casual when she'd never had breezy, casual sex in her life. "And you're going to be my transition guy, so it's all good."

"Your transition guy?" he repeated, seemingly not clear on the term.

She nodded and turned on her side to face Wes, wanting him to know that she wasn't looking for anything serious, that she didn't expect anything from him but great sex. No strings. No commitments. No promises. They'd part ways having gotten each other out of their systems, and she could get her head back into the dating game. It really was the perfect arrangement, for both of them.

She placed her hand on his chest, the skin warm beneath her palm. "I haven't been with anyone since Mitch," she told him, pushing the words out. Even though she didn't want to have this conversation with Wes, she needed to clarify her *transition guy* comment. "I've moved on emotionally, because let's face it, he was a lying, cheating, cock-sucking asshole." Damn, that felt good to say out loud.

Wes's deep, rumbling chuckle reverberated against her hand. "Personally, I never liked the guy. I always thought you were way too good for him."

She blinked at Wes in surprise, not sure what to make of his comment, or the fact that he'd even paid any attention to her relationship with Mitch.

"Umm, anyway, I figure it's time for me to get back on the horse again—"

"Or in this case, get back on the cock again?" he asked, his eyes glinting with humor as he traced the dip of her waist, then up the curve of her hip with his lazy fingers.

His sensual touch made her nipples pucker tighter and a liquid heat pool in her belly and lower. She fought the arousing distraction, at least until she was done explaining. "So, this thing between us . . . the sex, the boning," she added with a grin, just to inject some levity into the conversation as she slid a hand down his stomach to his semi-erect shaft and stroked him to full-fledge in her palm, "is all about having fun and enjoying an unemotional fling, without any expectations on either of our parts. I get that you're not a settling-down kind of guy, but you're the guy I want to have wild, anything-goes sex with before I get serious about dating again."

The look in his eyes was undecipherable, and his expression seemed . . . off, or maybe she was just imagining things or reading too much into his quiet demeanor. But he hadn't refused her idea, and she took that as a sign that he was totally on board with her proposition. What guy wouldn't be?

Done talking, she leaned closer and touched her lips to his. "Now that that discussion is out of the way, how do you feel about me getting you off just like this?" she asked, giving his stiff cock a long, slow tug as she kissed the corner of his mouth, then along his jaw before looking into his eyes again. "I've always wanted to watch a guy come in my hand."

His gaze grew hot, and after a hard thrust into her snug grasp, he unwrapped her fingers from his dick, brought her hand to his mouth, and licked her palm to make it slippery and wet. Then he put it back in place, his shaft even harder than it was a few seconds ago.

Still lying facing one another, he shoved his fingers into her hair and brought her mouth back to just beneath his. He lightly nipped at her bottom lip, then soothed the love bite with his tongue. "Fuck me in your fist, baby," he ordered in that dominant tone she was beginning to love. "Do it hard and slow. Make it as nice and tight as your pussy feels, because that's what I'm going to be imagining as you get me off."

And yeah, he kissed her with that dirty, filthy mouth. His lips pushed hers apart, and his tongue swept in to inundate her senses while she attempted to overwhelm his with the rhythmic jerk of her hand snug and slick around his girth. His tongue plundered as deep as his thrusts, and his hips started to move, pistoning faster, harder against her palm.

Masturbating Wes was the hottest thing she'd ever done to a man, making him wild with

CARLY PHILLIPS & ERIKA WILDE

nothing more than her hand providing the pleasure while he pumped uncontrollably, until abruptly, he tore his mouth from hers and pushed her onto her back, momentarily breaking the contact of her hand on his cock as he moved over her. He braced his hands on either side of her shoulders on the bed and poised his body above hers, the heavy tip of his shaft skimming along her belly.

"I'm so fucking close. Finish me off," he demanded harshly. "Do it. Make me come hard. *Now.*"

She took him in her palm again, realizing that he'd changed positions so that she could watch as he climaxed. And it didn't take long, just a few more tight strokes, and he growled and shuddered and threw his head back as his entire body began to shake . . . and she had a front-row seat to it all. The straining cords in his neck. His heaving chest. The rippling of his abs. The shallow jerking of his hips as he kept driving harder, faster, deeper into her fist.

And finally, she felt the pulsing along the underside of his erection right before his orgasm burst free, along with a long, hoarse groan. Hot spurts of thick, milky fluid erupted from his cock, surging as high as her breasts and eventually pooling onto her stomach. It was spectacular to watch him lose control and to know that he'd done so because of her.

A secret little smile touched her lips as he lowered himself on top of her, the sticky mess between them slickening their skin and making an even *bigger* mess.

She pressed against his shoulders, which did nothing to make him move. "Arggh, seriously, Wes?"

He chuckled and lifted his head from her neck, his lashes half-mast, his expression sated. "Yes, seriously. You wanted wild, anything-goes sex, and coming all over your tits and stomach definitely qualifies, and it was hotter than fuck."

Okay, she couldn't argue with that. Everything about what had just happened was emblazoned on her mind, an erotic fantasy for her to retrieve later when it was just her and Liam again.

He smiled down at her, slow and sexy, and she hated that her heart skipped a beat when nothing about her heart should have been involved in this fling. "Besides, cleaning up this mess gives us a great excuse to have shower sex. What do you say about that, Minx?"

Her inner hussy gave an enthusiastic *hell*

yeah, and Natalie grinned right back at him. "I'm totally in."

Chapter Eleven

WES WASN'T SURE why being Natalie's transition guy bothered him so much. But two days after their night together, on the drive to pick her up for the Sunday afternoon surprise birthday party for a friend that he'd asked her to accompany him to, he was still thinking about the fact that she was using him to get over her ex.

Okay, she hadn't said those words exactly, but the fact that she was using him to transition her way back into finding a suitable guy to date . . . he figured it was the same damn thing. Normally, the whole *let's have fun and not take things too seriously* rule was *his* mantra. Words he lived by when it came to all the women who'd passed through his life, since his high school days.

So, now that the situation was reversed and Natalie had laid out the terms of their affair, why did being relegated to being her fuck buddy make him feel so . . . annoyed?

God, it was all so confusing and ridiculous. As Connor or one of the other guys would say, he was acting like a fucking girl—wanting more time with Natalie, thinking about her when they weren't together, sending her amusing and sexy texts throughout the day and anxiously awaiting her witty responses.

One night of fucking his best friend's sister and his business adversary—the one woman he'd sworn he'd never touch that way—and he was like a goddamn puppy needing her attention, waiting for a pat on the head, a scratch behind the ear, or a freakin' belly rub. He smirked to himself at that latter thought, because judging by the hand job she'd given him two nights ago, he was pretty sure that Natalie would give *really* good belly rubs.

The navigation system in his car told him to turn down Belmont Avenue, cutting into his thoughts as he neared her condo. For as many times as she'd been to his place, he'd never been to hers. Never had a reason to. He knew from

Connor that after Natalie's breakup with Mitch, she'd bought the small two-bedroom condo on her own. It was located in a nice area of Roscoe Village where real estate held its appreciation, and resale value was something that would be important to her, being an agent, for the future, depending on how long she decided to hold on to the place.

He parked his vehicle in a lot for visitors and walked toward the building. It was the end of August, a little humid but a nice enough afternoon for a birthday gathering. Making his way up to the sixth floor, he found her unit and knocked on the door. She answered a few moments later, wearing a pretty but casual peach-colored dress with a band around the waist that was made of the same color of lace. The sleeves were short, the neckline appropriately modest, and the hem ended just above her knee. She'd left her hair down in soft waves, and her eyes looked even bluer than normal because of whatever she'd done with her makeup.

"Hey, beautiful," he said, resisting the urge to push her back into the condo and up against the wall so he could have his way with her before they left. Two fucking days, and he was dying to be inside her again. Was already counting down the hours until they could leave the party and he could get her naked and pinned beneath him.

Smiling, she gave him a quick, appreciative once-over, taking in his burgundy shirt and black jeans. "Hi, yourself, handsome. I'll try not to spill a drink on your pants tonight."

He chuckled at the reminder of her doing just that at his poker game . . . and what it had eventually led to. The best fucking sex of his life. Seriously. Nothing came close to what this woman did to him physically. He didn't want to think about how she was starting to tie him up in knots emotionally, because that was just too dangerous a place for him to go.

She opened the door wider and he walked inside, then followed her into the small living room. She was wearing a pair of shiny, high-heeled beige pumps, and predictably his eyes were drawn to the subtle sway of her hips and the way the material of her dress smoothed over her ass.

"You wearing panties beneath that dress?" Because as far as he could see, there were no telltale lines.

She gave him a cheeky smile over her

shoulder. "Yes, I'm wearing a g-string, so keep your dick in your pants."

Yeah, sure. Now that she'd put *that* hot mental image in his head, every time he looked at her ass, his horny dick was going to follow her around like a heat-seeking missile.

"Give me a sec," she said as she kept on walking toward another door that led into what looked like the master bedroom. "I need to grab my lipstick and purse, and then I'll be ready to go."

Once she disappeared into the room, he glanced around the place, which was smaller and more compact than he would have thought. From where he stood in the living room, he could see both bedroom doors, a main bathroom, and the connecting kitchen. The furnishings, though high quality, were just the essentials because there wasn't much extra room for anything more than the basics. The decor was clean and uncluttered and made up in neutral tones, with splashes of brighter colors thrown in to showcase a bit of Natalie's personality.

She returned a few minutes later, her lips now shiny with a peach-colored gloss that looked like candy he wanted to eat off her mouth. She adjusted the long strap of a beige purse over her shoulder and stopped in front of him, bringing with her the scent of something soft and flowery.

"Nice place," he said, meaning it. Despite the size, it was reflective of her.

"Thanks." She glanced around the living room, as if seeing it through his eyes. "It's small, but it's just me living here, so it's fine for now."

"A transition home?"

Oh, shit, did he really just go there? Did his subconscious just betray the fact that he was a tad bit annoyed being labeled her transition guy? Judging by the amused arch of her brow, yeah, she'd definitely caught on to his not-so-subtle gibe.

Instead of calling him on it, she shrugged it off. "I guess you could call it that. I don't intend to live here forever."

Just like she didn't intend to be with him forever.

Where the fuck did that thought come from? And why the hell did he feel as though he'd just been kicked in the stomach?

"I want a nice house someday," she went on, oblivious of the turmoil he was dealing with inside his chest. "But it doesn't make sense for me to buy one on my own. I'd like to think I'm going to meet someone who wants to get married, have kids, and live in the suburbs. Then I can sell this place."

Everything he'd *never* wanted. Her little spiel should have put things into perspective, but instead it made him feel oddly . . . alone. Which was exactly what he preferred, he quickly told himself. He wasn't interested in marriage, or even kids, not when he'd watched how ugly things had gotten between his parents, how a divorce had ripped apart their family, and how he, as a young preteen, had grown resentful and bitter toward his father for devastating Wes's mother and walking away to start a new life and a new family with the woman he'd been having an affair with.

And that's why Wes kept himself closed off to women. Not because the leaving had wrecked his mother emotionally but because his father's selfish choices had destroyed a part of Wes and had made him feel as though he hadn't been good enough for his dad to stay, or even worth him visiting after the nasty divorce.

Once his father was gone, Wes only knew that he never wanted to feel that kind of all-encompassing rejection from someone he'd loved ever again. And so he'd always avoided emotional ties with a woman, deliberately ending things before they could decide he wasn't boyfriend material or that he wasn't what they were looking for in a man.

It was easier and much less complicated that way, and he *liked* being a bachelor—free to come and go as he pleased, no drama in his life, and a little black book filled with plenty of females willing to enjoy a casual hook-up, no strings attached, all at a moment's notice. The arrangement had always worked for him, so why did he even care that Natalie wanted to get married, have a family, and live in the suburbs? He might not be cut out for wedded bliss, but he'd known Natalie for over twenty years, and while she'd been a pain in his ass most of that time, she certainly deserved to be some lucky man's wife, he told himself, forcefully ignoring the heavy sensation settling in the pit of his stomach like a rock.

"Hey, Wes, where did you go?"

Natalie's voice penetrated his thoughts, and he realized he was frowning and she was staring at him quizzically. He gave his head a shake, quickly reminding himself that this thing between them was all about mutually satisfying sex. It was what they both wanted and agreed upon. Hot, anything-goes fucking. For now, she was his, but what she did after the terms of their bet was fulfilled, and with whom, was none of his concern. Even if he didn't like the thought of her being with another man after him—someone nice, steady, and dependable . . . like Richard.

"Ready to get going?" he asked, because he was more than ready to leave his serious thoughts behind.

With a nod from her, they headed out of the building toward where he'd parked his car. He tucked her into the passenger-side seat of his sporty Audi Coupe, then got behind the wheel. Once they were on the road, Natalie turned toward him on the leather seat, the slight shift causing her dress to move up her smooth thighs a few tantalizing inches. "Tell me how you know the guy who is having the birthday so I know a little about him before we get there."

He welcomed the distracting conversation. "I met him about six years ago after he'd gone through a bad divorce, and I sold him a condo on Lake Shore Drive. We became good friends after that. His name is Jackson Stone . . . or rather, Kincaid, since he recently changed his last name." Wes was still getting used to that switch, even though he completely understood the reasons for his friend's choice.

"Why would he change his last name?" she asked curiously.

"He was illegally adopted as a newborn," Wes said, still a bit astounded by the story that Jackson had told him months ago. "He was a twin, and his birth mother sold him for drug money, so it was all very black market."

She gasped in shock. "Oh, my God."

Wes briefly glanced at Natalie, her eyes round and filled with disbelief. "Even being adopted, Jackson had a crappy life growing up, and when he found out from his aunt that he was illegally adopted, he had a PI search for his real family and found his three brothers. Mason, Levi, and his twin, Clay Kincaid."

"Wow," she said softly. "I take it they're all very close now?"

He nodded. "It took awhile for his siblings to come around, but yeah, they're all really nice guys, and Jackson finally feels like he fits into a family, which is why he changed his last name to Kincaid, since that's his legitimate birth one. He recently got married to a woman named Tara, who works as a bartender for the Kincaid brothers."

"The whole illegal adoption thing is fascinating, but I'm glad it worked out for him and he's with the family he always should have been with."

Wes silently agreed. "I'm happy for him, too. In fact, even though Clay is his twin, today's surprise party is all about Jackson because they wanted to do something special just for him."

As he continued the drive to Clay's house, where the party was being held, he gave Natalie a quick rundown on Jackson's brothers and their wives, all of whom he'd met at his friend's wedding to Tara a few months back. That way, she'd at least have some knowledge as to who was who before they arrived.

As the invitation had instructed, Wes parked on a side street so Jackson wouldn't recognize his car, and he walked the short distance with Natalie to Clay's house, located in a nice neighborhood in a suburb. Samantha answered the door, and after introductions, she ushered them out to the backyard deck to wait for Jackson's arrival, which gave Wes time to introduce Natalie to the people that he knew personally, which was mostly Jackson's new family—his brothers and their wives, and a few co-workers from Jackson's architectural firm.

Twenty minutes later, the man of the hour stepped through the glass slider to the backyard with his wife, Tara, beside him, where he was met with a loud chorus of "surprise!" And judging by the startled look on his face, he clearly hadn't been expecting a party in his honor.

The casual party got underway, with a bar set up for beer and mixed drinks, a DJ playing music, and a local restaurant that had catered in a buffet for dinner that included barbeque ribs, chicken, and an assortment of side dishes. At some point, the ladies gravitated together on the deck to talk about whatever women talked about, with Natalie included in the group since she'd hit it off with the Kincaid wives right from the start. The bunch of them were chatting and laughing as if they were all old friends. But then again, Natalie always did have an outgoing personality.

The men did the same, banding together and discussing mostly business-related stuff, and between all four Kincaid siblings, there was a wide range of careers to cover—bar owner, tattooist, cop, and architect. Toss in Wes's real estate background, and there was no lack of interesting conversation.

After a while, Samantha stepped out onto the deck with a happy, bright-eyed baby in her arms, Charlotte, who was about six months old, if Wes remembered correctly. Clay's wife joined the women again, and the conversation around Wes suddenly faded as he watched as Natalie asked to hold the little girl, and Samantha didn't hesitate to hand the baby over.

The expression on Natalie's face was soft and wistful as she talked to Charlotte and tickled her belly, and the infant bounced in her arms and waved her fists gleefully, making Natalie laugh. Gently, she caressed her hand over the wispy blond hair on Charlotte's head, then Natalie leaned in and gave the baby a sweet kiss on the temple.

That's when Natalie caught him watching, the look etching her features filled with unmistakable longing that said, *I want this so much.* Not with him, he knew, but with a man who could, and would, give her those things.

In that moment, Wes was grateful that his heart was concealed inside of his chest, because it suddenly felt heavy with a regret he'd never, ever experienced before. And he certainly didn't want to start thinking about what ifs right now. But all at once he was hyperaware that most everyone around him at this party was married and happy and starting families and moving on with their lives. Hell, even Mason's wife, Katrina, and Levi's wife, Sara, were walking around with noticeable pregnant bellies and glowing about it. And Wes was . . . right where he'd always been. Single, happy—which was relative to each person, he supposed—and swearing he didn't want to have anything to do with settling down.

"Uh, oh, are you feeling the urge to populate with some baby Sinclairs?" While Wes had been lost in his thoughts, Jackson had come up beside him and figured out what had ensnared his attention . . . Natalie holding a baby. He took a drink of beer from his bottle and glanced at his friend, giving him a droll smile. "Not even close."

Jackson studied him for a few moments longer before glancing back at the circle of women and speaking again. "You know, the whole marriage thing isn't as unpleasant as you might think."

Wes arched a brow. "This coming from the guy who went through a nasty divorce?"

His friend shrugged. "So I didn't get it right the first time, and looking back, I never should have married Collette, because I did it for the wrong reasons. But Tara . . . " A sappy smile transformed his expression. "She is everything I want and didn't know I needed. And so much more. But I suppose that's something you're just going to have to figure out for yourself."

Wes rolled his eyes in humor. "Okay, yeah, thanks for your words of wisdom." But he already knew they didn't apply to him. And especially not him and Natalie—his best friend's little sister and a woman who'd already set down strict guidelines for their affair, which didn't include anything other than getting laid regularly for the next two weeks.

"By the way, isn't that the brunette who was ignoring you that time we met for drinks over at the Popped Cherry?" Jackson questioned in a speculative tone.

Wes was surprised his friend remembered that evening. "Yes."

"And now she's dating you?" he asked incredulously. "How the hell did that happen?"

"She lost a bet we made, and now she owes me two weeks of her time." That was the nice, polite version.

"Jesus, Sinclair, you're resorting to bribing women now?" Laughter tinged Jackson's voice.

"Hardly. I've never had to bribe a woman for anything. Natalie lost, fair and square." He finished off the last of his beer. "So far, it's been . . . interesting."

Jackson scoffed. "A beautiful, sexy woman like that, and the only word you can come up with is *interesting*?"

Other words definitely came to mind to describe his time with Natalie so far . . . aggravating, frustrating, amusing, entertaining, and hot as hell. He couldn't ever remember having so much *fun* with a woman before. But then again, no other woman would have ever dared to follow through with the stunts that Natalie had that night at his poker game. And looking back at that evening, Wes realized for as exasperated as he'd been at the time, he now thought about it with a fond smile. It took a daring woman to provoke him the way she had, without fear of the consequences. A woman with ingenuity to keep him guessing, which was a huge turn-on. Being with Natalie was like a whirlwind, and he enjoyed that unpredictability more than he would have ever believed.

Jackson's wife, Tara, came up to them and

grabbed her husband's hand. "Hi, Wes," she said to him with a smile. "Do you mind if I steal Jackson away for a few minutes?"

"Of course not," Wes said graciously. "He is, after all, the birthday boy."

Jackson's eyes lit up hopefully, teasingly as he looked down at his wife. "Is this some kind of surprise present you can only give me in private?"

Tara batted his arm as a blush swept across her cheeks. "Behave yourself. You already got *that* present this morning."

Jackson chuckled. "Yeah, that was a fantastic way to start the day, but I'm not opposed to another one of those presents."

"*Stop*," Tara said, embarrassed but still laughing.

She pulled Jackson away, and since Wes didn't see Natalie around—last he'd seen of her she was heading into the house with Samantha and the baby—he ventured over to Clay to continue a conversation he'd been having with the other man about a commercial building in the city he was interested in purchasing to open another bar.

After a while, Jackson stood up in front of everyone with Tara by his side, stating he'd like everyone's attention. The guests in the backyard grew quiet, and Wes was surprised when Natalie came up beside him and slipped her arm into his as if she belonged there. As if it was the most natural thing in the world to be so . . . intimate with him in public.

As a standard rule, he didn't like clingy women—females who overstepped their boundaries or tried to cozy up to him outside of the bedroom. He didn't hold hands, and he didn't invite public displays of affection because it sent signals to the woman that they were an item and that she belonged to him when she really didn't. It was a perception he steadfastly avoided because it led to awkward misunderstandings in terms of their affair.

But having Natalie lightly curl her arm around his and press up against his side made him feel . . . protective of her. And a little possessive, too. It made his pulse pound with awareness, and when he glanced at her and she smiled at him in such a soft, sweet manner, all he could think about was how much he enjoyed being with her when they weren't trying to one-up each other. And how much he wanted her. How badly he ached to hear her soft moans of bliss when he sank deep inside her. How desperate he suddenly was to get her alone so he could slake this constant desire she aroused in him.

"Hey," he said, his voice lower and huskier than he'd intended. "Are you having a good time?"

"Yes," she replied with a genuine nod of pleasure. "Everyone here is so nice and friendly."

"Good." He slid his arm around her waist and pulled her even closer to his side, not questioning something that felt so *right* in the moment. She blinked up at him in surprise, but she didn't protest or pull away.

The sound of Jackson's voice redirected their attention to the other man.

"So, first of all, I want to thank everyone for being here today," he said, his statement genuinely heartfelt. "And I have to tell you that Tara gave me the best gift I could ever ask for on my birthday," he began, but his smartass brother, Mason, cut him off.

"She's going to finally release that ball and chain?" he called out.

Tara gave Mason a mock glare, and Jackson didn't hesitate to flip his brother off, which made most everyone laugh.

Then Jackson grinned. "No, she's pregnant and I'm going to be a dad."

The women in the area gasped in delight, and Wes even heard Natalie release a soft little sigh that he would have sworn was laced with envy. The guys congratulated Jackson, and a round of shots was poured to celebrate.

"I'm going to head over to the dessert table," Natalie said to Wes. "Samantha said she made everything, and those lemon cupcakes are calling my name."

"Okay. I'll be done here in a sec." Wes didn't want to be rude since someone had already put a shot glass of liquor into his hands. Clearly, he was expected to partake in the upcoming toast to Jackson's impending fatherhood.

Fifteen minutes later, he went in search of Natalie and found her sitting at one of the many tables that had been set up for the guests out in the yard. She was off to the side in an area that wasn't well lit, and she was all alone, but she smiled when she saw him coming.

He sat down in the folding chair next to hers, facing her, his back to the deck, where everyone else was hanging out. "What are you doing out here by yourself?"

"Just watching everything going on."

There was something emotional in her eyes, a longing he didn't address because he didn't know what to say, and he certainly had no reassurances for her. So, instead, he turned the conversation to a topic that was much safer, for both of them.

"How's the cupcake?" he asked as she picked up the last little section left on her plate with her fingers.

"Absolutely amazing. This is my second one," she admitted guiltily, and winced in chagrin for indulging. "*Please* take the last bite."

He grinned wickedly. "You gonna feed it to me?"

"Are you sure you want me to do that?" She flashed him a playful smile.

She didn't wait for his answer. Instead, she automatically lifted the dessert toward him, the devious look in her eyes warning Wes that he was most likely going to end up with cake and frosting smeared across his face.

Grabbing her wrist before she could reach him, he took control and turned things around on her. He brought her hand to his parted lips and pushed her fingers—and the bite of cup-cake—into his mouth. He ate the lemony

CARLY PHILLIPS & ERIKA WILDE

dessert, moaning in agreement with just how delicious it was. But he didn't let go of her wrist. Instead, he licked the sticky remnants of frosting from her fingers and nibbled on the tips before sucking two deep into his mouth. He swirled his tongue around the lengths then slowly pulled them back out again.

She groaned softly in the back of her throat. "You're giving me dirty ideas about what I'd like to do to you."

He liked the way that sounded. A lot. "Ummm . . . let me give you a few more," he murmured, and proceeded to slide her fingers in and out of his mouth, deliberately putting a whole slew of suggestive images into her head.

Her breathing quickly escalated. Her lashes fell half-mast, and her eyes flickered with unmistakable lust. "Oh, God . . .you need to stop."

Leisurely, he pulled her fingers from his mouth but didn't release her hand just yet. "Don't you want to know what I'm going to do with you when I get you alone?"

"Wes . . . " she whispered, looking and sounding completely torn as to whether she wanted to take the good girl route or the bad girl one.

He made the decision for her. "Let me show you."

Holding her heavy-lidded gaze, he slid his tongue down between her index and middle finger, gradually spreading them apart for his mouth, then swept his tongue along that sensitive webbing where the two fingers joined, just as he'd done the other night between her legs. The darkening of Natalie's gaze, the way she bit her bottom lip and squirmed on her chair told him that she was remembering every erotic detail of how he'd gone down on her. And fuck, he couldn't wait to do it again.

"I . . . I think we need to go," she said, her voice excruciatingly aroused.

He pulled her fingers away from his mouth but held on to her hand. "I agree." And so did his rapidly hardening dick. They needed to leave while he could still walk out without embarrassing himself.

They made their rounds and said their good-byes, and as soon as they were in his car and on the road back to her place, she reached over and ran her hand up the inside of his thigh, then traced the hard outline of his thickening cock pressing against the fly of his jeans.

He swallowed a needy groan and gave her a

quick, uncertain glance as she unbuttoned his jeans and began pulling down his zipper. *Oh, fuck.* "What are you doing?" he asked in a strangled voice while desperately trying to keep his eyes focused on driving.

She unfastened her seat belt and leaned over the console, her lips touching along his jaw and up to his ear as she took the stiff length of his dick in her soft hand and gave him a slow, tantalizing stroke that made him even harder. "All those dirty ideas you just gave me . . . I want to put to good use, right now. So, keep your eyes on the road and drive carefully, okay?"

Since speech was suddenly impossible, he could only answer with an eager nod.

Chapter Twelve

THE MOMENT NATALIE'S warm, wet mouth enveloped his shaft, Wes's stomach hollowed out and his entire body shuddered with a sudden, excruciating need he'd never experienced before. It had nothing to do with the fact that having a woman give him a blow job while he was driving was a first for him— one of those hot fantasies he'd imagined as a teenager and had hoped for as an adult but had never found a woman brazen enough to do— but that undeniable *need* had everything to do with the woman herself.

For years he'd fought his attraction to Natalie, for various valid reasons, but he was beginning to wonder if, despite keeping her at arm's length emotionally, she'd somehow gotten under his skin any way. And now that they had free reign to give in to every one of their desires for one another, everything he'd held back and those deep, buried feelings he'd harbored for Natalie were becoming a reality he could no longer ignore.

The thought scared the hell out of him, and he was eternally grateful when she wrapped her lips tight around the base of his cock and slowly worked her way back up to the head again, dissolving every worry in his mind except for the absolute pleasure of her generous, ravenous mouth working his dick over. She put her tongue to good use, licking him from root to tip and swirling it around the swollen, sensitive crown, taunting and tormenting him and keeping him right on the edge of release, which was nothing less than he'd expect from the tease. And for now, he allowed her be the one in control.

Concentrating on the road took effort, as did the drive back to her place. He had to grit his teeth more than once, and both of his hands gripped the steering wheel like a lifeline as she took him all the way to the back of her throat and made a purring sound that vibrated along the length of his shaft. Her head bobbed in his lap, her silky hair spilling across his abdomen, while her decadent mouth sheathed him again and again, sucking repeatedly, but always careful to pull back and slow down when he was only a few strokes away from coming.

When he reached her place, he parked his car in the very back of the lot, where it was dark and secluded. He shut off the engine with an abrupt twist of his wrist, and before Natalie could lift her head, he burrowed his hand into her hair, twisting the strands tight around his fingers, and guided her mouth back over his driving cock. With a soft moan, she went back down on him willingly, swallowing him greedily, even when he pushed so fucking deep he felt her constrict around the head before her throat opened up to take more of him.

The avid, eager sounds Natalie made spurred him on as he continued to fuck her lush mouth. He was so aroused he ached from his thighs to his belly, the muscles in his stomach flexing as the tension building inside of him finally reached that breaking point. It was all so good, *so fucking good*, and there was nothing he could do but surrender to the intense climax throbbing its way through his shaft.

While his strangled groans filled the small

confines of the car, his head fell back against the headrest, and he squeezed his eyes shut as his hips arched off the seat, instinctively thrusting every inch of his cock between her soft lips. With a sharp gasp and a guttural shout, he came, pumping hot and hard down her throat. Waves of pleasure rolled through him, knocking the breath out of his lungs, until the last spasm of release shook his entire body.

When he finally came back to his senses, he found Natalie smiling at him, the dim lighting in the car enabling him to see the pleased look in her eyes as she ran her tongue along her bottom lip. "That was so hot," she murmured.

A fucking understatement. All he could manage was an appreciative grunt for a reply, and with fumbling fingers, he eased his dick back into his jeans.

"Want to come up for a nightcap?" she offered.

She'd definitely taken the edge off for him, but he wasn't done with Natalie for the evening, and there was no way he was going to pass up any opportunity to spend more time with her. "Only if that is code for getting you naked and having my way with you."

She laughed huskily. "That sounds *really*

good to me."

He escorted her up to her place, and as soon as they were in her condo and the door was shut and locked behind them, she set her purse down on a small table and started to walk away from him, toward the kitchen.

Before she had the chance to leave the entryway, he snagged her around the waist with his arm and pulled her backside flush to his front. "Where are you going, Minx?" he asked against her ear.

He felt her shiver against him. "I thought we *really* might have a drink so you could . . . you know, have some time to recharge your batteries."

Did she honestly think he needed downtime before he could get it up for her twice in a row? Just holding her this close and inhaling her alluring feminine scent, as well as feeling the soft curve of her bottom pressed up against his groin, already had him getting nice and stiff again.

He rolled his hips against hers, making sure she felt the hard length of his erection along the crease of her ass. "The only thing that is going to *recharge my batteries* is you."

"Oh," she said on a soft exhale.

"Yeah, *oh*." He chuckled as he walked her in the direction of her small living room, then released her. His hands went to the zipper at the back of her dress and pulled it all the way down to the base of her spine, then he pushed the material off her shoulders so it fell to the floor at her feet.

She started to turn around, but he put his hands on her arms and stopped her. "Don't move," he ordered in a firm tone. "Stay right where you are and take off your bra and panties and shoes."

While she did exactly as he asked, and he was able to watch, he also stripped out of his own clothes so that getting naked was completely out of the way and he could fuck her without breaking the moment. He also donned one of the condoms he'd tucked into his wallet before leaving his house today so that wouldn't be an issue, either.

Gently pushing her hair off to one shoulder so the right side of her neck was exposed, he closed the distance between them again and used the same arm around her waist to anchor her up against his naked body, loving how she fit so perfectly against him. As if she was designed specifically for him. He placed his free hand at her throat, and with a gentle pressure, he tipped her head back so it was resting on his shoulder and he could place hot, damp kisses along her neck.

She moaned his name like a plea as he licked across her skin. Her knees started to shake, and he felt her stomach tremble where his other hand was splayed.

"Tell me what you want," he rasped into her ear, willing to give her anything she asked for. Anything she desired.

Her backside squirmed shamelessly against his hips, and she reached back and gripped his thighs with her fingers. "Touch me . . . between my legs."

"Take my hand and show me where," he demanded.

She didn't hesitate to push the arm around her waist down toward her mound, then guided his long fingers through the swollen lips of her sex, where she was hot and slick and so fucking wet he had to swallow back a groan.

He stroked her drenched pussy and sank his teeth lightly into the side of her neck, smiling as she jerked back against him. "This for me, baby?"

"All for you," she confirmed with a delirious nod of her head. "Sucking you off made my pussy weep for you. Made me so worked up and needy . . . "

She sounded so breathless and desperate, and wanting to soothe her ache, Wes turned her around and backed her up a few steps, until the support of the wall held her upright. Her eyes were glassy, aroused, and when he pushed two fingers deep inside of her and pressed his thumb against her clit, she didn't hesitate to chase after what her body craved.

Closing her eyes, she grabbed his upper arms and undulated her hips, pushing them against the firm pressure he was applying between her legs, where he was rubbing against that hard nub at the hood of her sex. Her breasts swayed as she rocked her body, her nipples hard and tight. Then a soft little sob of frustration broke from her lips, as if she couldn't quite grasp what she needed so badly.

He wedged a knee between her legs, widening them to give him more room to pleasure her. "Come on, sweetheart," he murmured, doubling his efforts to get her off. "Ride my hand. Fuck my fingers. You're almost there."

She shook her head frantically, and then she opened her beautiful eyes and looked at him with such unabashed desire and longing, unlike anything that had ever been directed at him before. If that wasn't enough to shake him up, then she completely slayed him with her next words.

"No . . . I need *you*," she said softly, adamantly. "Fuck me, Wes. I need it as hard and deep as you can go. Only you . . . "

Jesus, she looked so exposed emotionally, so vulnerable. And he wanted to give her everything she wanted, everything she needed . . . except physical pleasure was all he had to offer.

"Where should I fuck you, baby?" he asked huskily. "Should I bend you over the end of the couch? Or push you to your hands and knees and take you on the floor? Or how about right here, up against the wall?"

She whimpered anxiously. "Anywhere. Just do it. Now. *Please*."

And that's exactly what he did. He hooked one of her thighs as high as it could go on his hip, and wanting as much leverage as he could get to fill her up so she'd never be able to tell where he ended and she began, he issued his next order. "Wrap your legs tight around my waist and lock your ankles behind my back," he said gruffly, and she obeyed, climbing him like a proverbial tree. The grip of her thighs was strong and tight, as was the way she locked her hands around his neck.

Holding her bottom in his hands, he angled her hips, lined up his cock to her entrance, and with one hard thrust, he was balls deep inside her slick heat and had her shoulders pinned to the wall. If he'd had his choice, he would have made this a slow, hard fuck. But she was already struggling to move on his dick, trying to rock his shaft into her deeper, if that was even possible.

The wet heat of her pussy, the unrelenting friction of her body clenching around his dissolved any semblance of control he had left and gave him no choice but to move, to instinctively pump into her, again and again. She sank her teeth into the side of his neck, sending a jolt of lust straight down to his cock, and *fuck*, he knew he was only a few short strokes away from exploding inside her.

"So . . . damn . . . close." His lips parted on a quick intake of breath as she started to claw at his back with her nails, the stinging sensation adding to the fire in his belly, the rhythmic pulsing in his dick. "I want to feel you come all over my cock. *Need* it so fucking bad." The words came out of his mouth, uncensored, revealing more than he'd ever intended.

"Yes . . . I want that, too," she panted frantically. "So much."

And then she chanted in his ear, "*Harder, faster, deeper*," and he fulfilled her demands, shoving her tight against the wall and pinning her there as he surged against her, burying himself to the hilt over and over and making her feel *everything*. The intense heat. The infinite desire. The overwhelming need.

She moaned his name as he felt the fluttering of her muscles squeeze around his dick, the rippling sensation of her impending orgasm pulling at him like an undertow. He lifted his head, watching as she gave herself over to her climax, *to him*, so wild and gorgeous, so strong and confident and passionate, and holding nothing back as she rode his cock straight into ecstasy.

Her open, uninhibited response was the most stunning, beautiful sight he'd ever seen.

Another hard, deep thrust and he was right behind her, the pleasure so intense, so intimate and pure it forced him to acknowledge the truth. That no one had ever made him feel like this . . . this completeness, this connection, this reality.

No one . . . until Natalie.

✧   ✧   ✧

A FEW WEEKS ago, if someone would have told Natalie that she'd have hot, mind-altering, out-of-this-world sex with Wes Sinclair, her archenemy since childhood, then would be sitting on her living room sofa eating a grilled cheese sandwich with him afterward, she would have died laughing at the absurdity of such a suggestion.

Yet here they were, sitting side by side—him sprawled out wearing just his jeans and her cross-legged in a tank top and pajama shorts—the two of them indulging in a late-night snack together after an amazing round of up-against-the-wall sex and an orgasm that had nearly left her comatose. Not that she was complaining, she thought, as a warm flush suffused her cheeks.

"Are you blushing?" Wes asked playfully, his gaze fixed on her face.

"No," she denied much too quickly, and returned her attention to the second half of her grilled cheese sandwich.

"I think you are," he persisted as he finished

off the last of his own sandwich before adding insult to injury. "Who knew that little Natalie Prescott could talk so dirty?"

Clearly, she wasn't a prude, but there was something about Wes that tapped into a part of her she'd never known existed, until sex with him had unleashed a floodgate of indecent behavior. Spankings, sucking him off in his car on the drive home, begging him to fuck her . . .

She felt her skin heat even more when she realized the things that had come out of her mouth less than a half an hour ago. "You're a horrible influence. You seem to bring out the bad girl in me."

"I like it," he said, his low, husky voice equivalent to an intimate caress. "Am I the only one who's gotten to play with your inner bad girl?"

She ate her last bite of grilled cheese, which gave her a few extra seconds to consider her answer. "Yes, but don't let it go to your big, fat head."

He laughed and looked way too smug anyway. No big shock there.

"Mitch wasn't the dirty-talking type?" he asked curiously as he relaxed more fully into the corner of the couch.

She couldn't believe they were having this conversation about her ex, but Wes looked genuinely interested, and honestly, what did it matter if she discussed the less-than-exciting sex life she'd had with Mitch now that they were no longer together?

"No, he was strictly vanilla. I'm sure if I ever asked him to fuck me, he would have been scandalized and would have kicked me out of his bed." When she realized what she'd just said, she gave Wes a wry smile. "Oh, wait, he *did* do that."

Wes didn't even crack a smile at her attempt at a joke. Instead, his gaze was serious and compassionate as it held hers. "You were obviously way too much for him to handle."

She frowned, her stomach pitching with insecurities and doubts. "Am I that much of a pain in the ass that he'd have an affair with another woman?" Had she been too ambitious, too driven, too focused on work as Mitch had accused her of being? Too high maintenance?

"Natalie, that's not what I meant," he said quickly, and when she continued to stare at him quietly, desperate for an explanation, he gave her one. "I told you I never liked the guy, that I thought you were too good for him, and it's true. From what I saw, he was uptight, insecure, and so fucking needy, and you were always trying to please him. And because there is just no pleasing a self-centered guy like that, no matter what you do or how much time you spend with him, you always seemed stressed out."

"I was," she admitted as she drew her legs up onto the couch. "The balance between work and our relationship was exhausting. And frustrating."

He stretched his arm across the back of the sofa, his fingers playing with her hair. "If any guy can't handle the fact that you're a strong, intelligent, career-minded woman, then he's a fucking pussy and you're better off without him."

The corner of her mouth twitched with a smile. It felt good to hear someone else validate her emotions when a part of her *had* wondered if she'd been to blame.

"I just never expected to be cheated on," she said, hating that part the most. The heartbreaking betrayal and feeling like a fool. "Why not just break up with me and date someone else? We talked about getting married and having a family, and if he didn't want that with me, or I made him so unhappy, then why stay and be miserable?"

Wes let out a caustic laugh. "Wish I knew the answer to that. Believe me, I used to wonder the same thing about my father. If he was that unhappy, why didn't he just divorce my mother? Instead, he got caught in a lie, and when the truth came out about the affair, he blamed my mother . . . for not being there for him. For not giving him what he needed. Everything was all her fault, even though he was the one who'd fucked around."

She heard the bitterness in Wes's voice, and her heart ached for him. He'd been young when his parents had split, but he'd been good friends with Connor by then, and Natalie remembered how hard the breakup had been on him. But this was the first time he'd ever talked about it, and he obviously needed to release a lot of pent-up anger over what had happened and how it had affected him.

"If it wasn't bad enough that my father had torn my mother down emotionally, he dragged her through a nasty divorce, gave her a shitty settlement, and turned his entire family and their friends against her so she had no one to turn to." His jaw clenched tight, and his brows furrowed with contempt. "Of course, the asshole gave my mother minimal child support and thought that would make up for the fact that he was a shit father who turned his back on his son, as well."

Seeing the real, tangible anguish on Wes's face, she knew without a doubt that this was his reason for avoiding serious relationships. For him, he'd seen and been through the worst of them. "It's not always that way."

He stared at her in disbelief. "You can honestly say that after what you went through with Mitch? What he did to you?"

God, Wes was so cynical, but she knew that everyone handled their emotions differently. That everyone had their own reasons for making the choices they did. And just because Wes had sworn off committed relationships because of his father's actions and the pain they had caused, it didn't mean that Natalie felt the same. She definitely hated what she'd lost with Mitch—the possibility of marriage and a family. But she didn't hate that she'd lost *him*. No, him getting caught with another woman had been a blessing in disguise. Natalie was no longer stifled by Mitch's demands and expectations or feeling torn over having a career she loved.

And just because a relationship with Mitch hadn't worked out, it didn't mean she was going to let that particular heartbreak taint her belief in love and happily-ever-after. Her parents were proof that marriages worked, that two people could argue, fight, and compromise and still be true to the other. Out of love, mutual respect, and trust.

But she didn't expect Wes to understand or even accept *her* reasons when they had such different views. And the only thing she could do was make light of the situation, to bring in humor and sexy times to diffuse the heated conversation and alleviate his defensive mood.

Crawling over the one couch cushion separating them, she straddled his lap, drawing his attention to the fact that she wasn't wearing a bra and her nipples were already tight and hard against the thin cotton fabric. Distracting him further, she skimmed her fingers across his chest, down his deliciously firm abs, and followed that light trail of hair that disappeared into the waistband of his jeans.

"Haven't you heard that saying that sometimes you have to kiss a lot of frogs before you find your prince?" She asked the question playfully, but it was also the best answer she could give him as to why she hadn't given up on finding a man who'd also, eventually, become her lifelong partner.

It took him a few extra seconds, but he finally, reluctantly lifted his gaze from her breasts and quirked an eyebrow at her. "Are you calling me a fucking frog?" he asked incredulously.

She laughed, because she could see the humor glimmering in the depths of his gaze, and that's exactly what she'd been aiming for. "Frog ... toad." She shrugged as she unsnapped the button to his jeans. "Whichever you prefer."

He secured his hands tight around her waist and tipped her back so she was lying on the sofa. Quickly, he reversed their positions so that he was the one straddling her hips. "First, I'm your transition guy," he grumbled as he shoved the hem of her tank top all the way up to her chin, exposing her bare breasts to his hot gaze. "And now I'm a goddamn frog?"

His tone was teasing, but what she wouldn't do for him to be that prince who swept her away. He possessed all the qualities needed— the honesty, the integrity. He was protective and even sensitive, though she knew he'd never admit it. But despite all that, he wasn't on the market, and he never would be. If she'd had any doubts whatsoever about his availability—and, of course, she hadn't—he'd made his views on relationships and marriage and the reasons behind them crystal clear tonight.

There was no use pining over something she couldn't have or change, so she took what she could, which was enjoying their frenemies-with-benefits arrangement.

"Frogs aren't all that bad," she told him as he fondled her breasts and plucked at her sensitive nipples while she slid her hands up his jean-clad thighs to the noticeable bulge in his pants.

He didn't look convinced. "How so?"

"They have very long, agile tongues," she said, having intimate knowledge of just how *exceptionally* well Wes knew how to use his. "And really, in the scheme of things, that's all that matters."

"I couldn't agree with you more." He flashed her a wicked grin as he lowered his head toward her breasts. "In fact, I'm gonna show you just how agile this tongue can be."

And over the course of the next hour, much to her pleasure and delight, he did just that.

Chapter Thirteen

"**I** HAVE TO say, getting laid on a regular basis has improved your mood immensely."

"What?" Natalie didn't know whether to laugh or glare at Richard, who was seated across from her at the cafe where they were having lunch together. "How has my mood improved? And I didn't realize my mood was an issue *before* getting laid on a regular basis."

He chuckled as he cut into his grilled halibut. "A week and a half of doing the dirty with Mr. Big Shot, and you're so much more relaxed and calm. You're not as stressed or on edge, or neurotic about being busy twenty-four seven and chasing after clients and building your little empire. In fact, I'd go so far as to say that

CARLY PHILLIPS & ERIKA WILDE

you've become quite flexible, and I don't mean in just a physical way," he added with a cheeky wink.

Natalie experienced a moment of panic as his words sank in, the cobb salad on her plate suddenly forgotten as her mind did a quick, screeching rewind. Yes, it had been ten days since she'd lost the bet to Wes. Ten days of making her jump through hoops to "pay up" on her lost wager as agreed—because let's face it, Wes wasn't going to let her off easy, even if she was putting out for him—but rewarding her in the hottest, most satisfying ways each and every time. But had she gotten so caught up in *Wes* that she'd gotten soft and her career had begun to suffer?

That dismay expanded in her chest. She'd had a few impressive sales since their bet, but what if she wasn't doing all she could to build her client base because she was distracted by sex on the brain? What if she was slipping and her focus had shifted to something, or rather, *someone*, at the cost of not accumulating more listings than she already had? What if she was falling for Wes, an unattainable man, at the expense of working toward her goal of being a well-respected broker? And what if . . .

"Jesus, Natalie," Richard said, yanking her out of her frantic thoughts. "Calm down. You're on the verge of hyperventilating."

Yes, her heart was racing, and she was breathing as though she'd just finished a marathon. "Can you blame me? You just told me that I'm calm and relaxed and not pursuing clients twenty-four seven, which means I'm not working like I should. That I'm missing opportunities. And flexible? What the hell is that supposed to mean?"

Richard rolled his eyes, pegging *her* as the drama queen she clearly was being. "Calm and relaxed, meaning you're finally enjoying life outside of work. And flexible, meaning you're not so uptight and rigid about your schedule."

She still didn't get it. "And why is that a good thing?" she asked, her voice pitching higher than normal.

Richard reached across the small table and placed his hand over hers and waited for her to look him in the eyes. "Because you're finding a balance with Wes and making work and play mesh on a daily basis. Instead of *all* work and no play."

She shook her head in denial. "There shouldn't be a 'balance' with Wes." Her job, her career, needed to be a priority right now. "He's my transition guy, remember?"

"I'm thinking he's becoming a lot more than that," he pointed out quietly. "This is the happiest I've seen you since . . . dare I say, since Mitch."

No, no, no, no *no*. She chanted the words in her head, but her traitorous heart was saying, yes, yes, yes, yes, *yes*.

Richard squeezed her hand. "I know you love your job. I know you want to be successful, and you will be. You've got a headhunter pursuing you for a reputable real estate firm in Atlanta, and that wouldn't be happening if you'd been sitting on your pretty little ass doing nothing."

She still hadn't made a firm decision about the job offer in Atlanta and had put off thinking about it until she'd fulfilled the terms of her bet with Wes. Which was incredibly stupid, considering what the move could mean to her future. And her career.

"*But*," Richard went on, "don't be so quick to walk away from something, or someone, that could mean more to you than a job."

Natalie's head began to throb, and she pressed her fingertips to her temples. "Wes isn't that someone," she said, hating the way her heart squeezed at those words. "I know he'll always be a part of my life because he's my brother's best friend, but this thing between us right now? We both know it's temporary." And she wasn't going to walk away from a solid job offer for a man who wouldn't, and couldn't, give her the commitment she needed.

Richard sighed and let it go. "We need to finish up lunch so we can head over to the Chamber of Commerce for the networking session. It starts in about half an hour."

She nodded, thankful that Richard was dropping the subject of Wes. But her emotions were already in turmoil, and the fact that Wes could affect her so profoundly in a mere ten days wasn't a good sign. This thing between them was supposed to be a fun, no-strings-attached fling, but somewhere along the way she realized she'd gone and done something incredibly foolish. Something she couldn't take back, no matter how hard she tried.

She'd always had feelings for Wes, but now she'd fallen hard for a man who would never love her back, and there was no doubt in her mind that by the time their fourteen days were over and they went their separate ways, she was going to end up with another broken heart.

Except this time, she had a feeling it wouldn't be so easy to repair.

"I CAN'T BELIEVE you're bailing on me," Wes said, talking to Max on his cell phone as he walked down the street toward the Joy District Restaurant and Bar, where the afternoon Chamber of Commerce networking session was being held.

"You know how much I hate those things," Max grumbled as an excuse.

"And you think I don't?" Business mixers were probably Wes's least favorite thing to do—right up there with eating Brussels sprouts and taking out the trash—but since he always managed to drum up useful contacts and increase his client base, he considered them a necessary evil.

The events were boring, he was forced to make small talk with other business associates, and inevitably he'd get hit on by some woman looking for a prime piece of real estate—*wink, wink*. The latter he admitted to taking advantage of a time or two, but since his bet with Natalie, he hadn't given any other woman a second thought. Quite the novelty for him, but he wasn't complaining considering the past ten days had been nothing short of entertaining, enjoyable, and satisfying, more than just physically.

"You told me that Natalie was going to be there," Max said, cutting into his thoughts. "I'm sure you can think of something ridiculous to make her do that'll ruffle her feathers."

Wes smirked. Max was, of course, referring to the bet and the many outrageous things he'd already asked Natalie to do. Like getting on the Centennial Wheel, and a few other straightforward requests, like making his dinner, doing his wash, and cleaning his house, which had been particularly fun for him since he'd requested that she wear the French maid outfit again, which she hadn't kept on for long.

The poker game had been the highlight, though nobody knew what came *after* he'd called it quits, and they never would. He wasn't one to kiss and tell, and he'd never exploit his affair with Natalie that way. And yeah, he didn't want to have to deal with Connor blowing a gasket if he ever discovered that Wes had been sleeping with his sister for nearly two weeks— never mind that Natalie was a grown woman and *she'd* been the one to suggest the fling.

Wes understood it was a Bro Code kind of thing—*thou shall not mess around with your best friend's sister because it could potentially ruin the friendship*—but what Connor didn't know wouldn't hurt him, or their business or personal relationship. As long as it stayed that way, they were fine.

He hung up the phone with Max and continued toward the Joy District, his mind playing over the highlights of the past ten days with Natalie. Who knew that a lost wager could lead to so many delightful possibilities? Like daring Natalie to perform some of the more outrageous sex acts in the *Kama Sutra*, which had led to a lot of laughing, swearing, and eventually, moans of pleasure when they discovered a few new positions that culminated into some intense orgasms.

And this past weekend, he'd made her wash his car with nothing but a white T-shirt on top, sans bra, that Wes made sure got nice and wet so he could enjoy the outline of those gorgeous breasts and tight nipples pressing against the clinging fabric. Not to mention the way those full mounds had bounced as she scrubbed the hood of his Audi or how her short shorts had ridden up and revealed her smooth ass cheeks when she bent over to dip the sponge into the soapy water. Yeah, total fantasy material.

True to her promise, everything he'd asked for, every challenge or dare he'd issued, Natalie had performed without complaint. He loved that she was so adventurous. So fearless. So willing to be bold and brazen with him.

He headed into the restaurant and rode the elevator up to the roof deck, where the networking mixer was being held in an outdoor setting overlooking the city. The gathering was already in full swing, with drinks and appetizers being served and business professionals mingling.

The prerequisite sticky name tag was affixed to his shirt, and he picked up a beer from the bar. As Wes made his way through the function, he kept an eye out for Natalie while stopping along the way to say hello to colleagues and acquaintances. He shook hands, passed out business cards, and had conversations with people in his industry. A solid half hour passed of schmoozing and making new contacts before he heard familiar feminine laughter that made his pulse jolt in awareness. Everything else around him faded away as he turned his head toward the sound he'd come to adore.

He smiled when he saw Natalie, looking sweet but incredibly sexy in a fitted beige skirt that was tight enough to ensure that she was wearing one of her g-strings beneath, and a mint-colored silk blouse that looked prim and proper. Except now Wes had intimate knowledge of what she wore beneath her business attire—enticing, tempting, dick-teasing lingerie.

She laughed again, the tone soft and intimate and flirtatious, and since it wasn't directed at Wes like it normally was, he glanced at who she was with. Two guys he didn't recognize and Richard, whom she was standing way too close to and was now smiling up at as he said something to her.

An unexpected wave of jealousy swept though Wes and settled into a tight knot in his gut, followed by a surge of possessiveness. Without questioning this unexplainable need he suddenly had to stake his claim, he excused himself from his current conversation and walked over to Natalie's group, just as she hooked her arm through Richard's and made a comment that had the two men standing across from her chuckling.

She's mine. She's all fucking mine, he wanted to roar like a goddamn Neanderthal. Instead, he somehow, someway, maintained his composure, though the tight frown that had furrowed between his brows remained. It was his only way to get his message across to these clowns that Natalie wasn't up for grabs ... *at least for another four days,* an inner voice in his brain reminded him.

Fuck you, conscience ... for pointing out how little time he had left with Natalie. But for that short duration that she still belonged to him, he realized he didn't want to share her with another guy. Not her smiles. Not her laughter. Not her flirtatious banter.

Richard saw him approaching first, and the corner of the man's mouth quirked with amusement. Wes didn't know what was so fucking funny, and the other man's levity only provoked his inner alpha male. Richard lightly jabbed Natalie in the side as she was talking in an animated fashion to the other men. Once he had her attention, Richard nodded in Wes's direction and said something he couldn't hear.

Natalie turned her head just as he arrived, her eyes widening in genuine surprise. "Wes!" She let go of Richard's arm. "I wasn't sure you were going to make it."

She'd asked him earlier in a text if he'd planned on coming to the event, and he hadn't given her a definitive answer because he'd had a meeting with a client right before this get-together and wasn't sure how long it would last.

"I'm here now," he said, his voice tight as he encompassed all three guys in a quick glance. "Afternoon, gentlemen."

"Hey, Wes," Richard said with an engaging smile that only irritated Wes more *because* of how friendly it was. "It's good to see you again."

"Same here," Wes lied, and made sure that his vise-like handshake sent a loud and clear message to the other man to keep his goddamn hands off Natalie.

Natalie gave him a concerned look, as if she was trying to figure out why he was being so abrupt, but she didn't call him on it. Instead, she gestured to the two guys standing across from her. "Let me introduce you to Dale and Jake, who are relatively new reps at First American Title."

Both men immediately whipped out business cards, and because Wes didn't want to look like a complete jackass, he accepted both contacts and gave them the same assertive handshake as he'd given Richard.

"Anything you need or we can help you with, don't hesitate to call either one of us or drop us an email," Dale said amicably.

In the realty business, title companies were an important part of the selling process. Wes had reps he already worked with, but it never hurt to have a few other contacts in his back pocket. Except at the moment, he wasn't feeling very chatty or cordial. He gave them a brief thank you and glanced back at Natalie, who had a *what the hell is wrong with you?* expression on her face.

"Can I have a moment alone with you, *sweetheart?*" Wes asked, making sure to put the emphasis on the pet name.

"Of course, *honey,*" she parried right back as she batted her lashes impudently at him. "Excuse us, please," she said to the three other guys.

With a possessive hand holding Natalie's arm, he guided her out of the event. There was no private place to have a conversation, and as soon as he saw the EXIT sign over the door leading to the stairwell, he headed there. He doubted anyone would be taking a climb up to the rooftop when there was an elevator available.

As soon as the door closed behind them, he backed Natalie up against the concrete-block wall and flattened his hands on either side of her shoulders to make sure she couldn't go anywhere, not without going through him first.

Annoyance flashed in her eyes. She opened her mouth to say something, most likely a smartass remark, but Wes took her face in his hands, tipped her head back, and cut her off with a hot, hard, dominant kiss.

Chapter Fourteen

NATALIE MOANED AS Wes's mouth claimed hers hungrily, greedily. His tongue pushed past her lips, and she didn't hesitate to invite him in deeper. Her fingers fisted in his dress shirt, not to push him away but to keep him close, to make sure he could feel that she was kissing him back with as much passion as she felt coursing through him.

Passion . . . and possession.

The two emotions were not mutually exclusive, and she couldn't deny that a part of her reveled in this aggressive side to Wes, mainly because of what had driven him to put his stamp of ownership on her. His kiss was laced with the hot taste of jealousy, and it thrilled her to know that she could have that kind of effect on him, a man who'd always had such a cavalier attitude toward women.

Judging by his abrupt, less-than-friendly behavior back at the event, cavalier was the last word she'd use to describe his feelings. Yet she was also smart enough to know that this covetous kiss didn't change anything between them. It didn't negate the fact that this affair between them had an end date, and it wasn't a promise of a future. She'd be a fool to believe that was even a possibility with him.

When he finally lifted his mouth from hers, he was breathing hard and she could feel the tension vibrating off his body.

She exhaled to calm her racing heart, then reached up to grab his wrists and pulled his hands away from her face. "What the hell, Wes?" she demanded, her tone exasperated.

His jaw clenched tight with displeasure, and he jammed his hands on his hips. "Those guys were flirting with you."

"They were being *friendly*," she said reasonably.

"Same fucking thing," he growled irritably.

She rolled her eyes at him.

"Don't fucking mock me."

She intentionally smirked, just to see his

eyes flare with frustration. "I can't help it. You're acting like a jackass."

He huffed out a breath, and damn if she didn't think he looked kinda adorable. "Yeah, well, I don't appreciate Richard being so *friendly* with you."

She had to swallow back a burst of laughter. "Are you serious right now, Sinclair?"

"The guy provokes me without saying a word, and I *know* he's doing it deliberately." He jammed his fingers through his hair and started to pace in the small area.

"He's not provoking you," she said, then realized that was a lie. "Okay, maybe he is. A little. But it's not because he's in some kind of turf war with you over me."

He scoffed at her. "You obviously don't know men and how they think."

She snickered to herself. "I know how *Richard* thinks, and it's not about getting *me* naked but rather seeing *you* naked."

Abruptly, he stopped pacing, and for a moment he looked dumbfounded by her comment, then his face scrunched up in confusion. "What?"

As fun as it was to see Wes suffer, he was about to learn the truth about her good friend.

"Richard is gay, Wes. He likes guys, not girls. In fact, he thinks you're kinda hot and that you have a nice ass."

Wes's eyes grew huge as realization dawned. "I do *not* need to know that he stares at my ass."

She grinned and moved away from the concrete wall. "He's just pushing your buttons because you're being all territorial and trying to stake your claim like a He-Man. I'm surprised you didn't whip out your penis for a dick-measuring contest back there, though I'm sure Richard would have enjoyed that."

Gaze narrowed, he stalked toward her. "I'll show you *staking my claim*."

Before she realized what he intended, he hefted her over his shoulder, caveman style. Then he was jogging down the flight of stairs, jarring her body with every step he took.

She gasped in shock, unable to believe he'd do something so outrageous. "Wes! Stop!"

Of course, he didn't listen, just kept spiraling his way down to the ground floor, carrying her as if he was used to hauling around an extra hundred and forty pounds over his shoulder. Since he didn't seem inclined to let her go, and they were getting closer to the exit, she threatened him with the one thing all guys weren't willing to give up.

"If you don't put me down right now, before we step out onto the street, your dick isn't
going to get anywhere near my pussy tonight!"
She winced at just how high-pitched her voice
had gotten and hoped to God no one but Wes
had heard her potty mouth.

Another effortless jog down a flight of
stairs. "Baby, you know just how persuasive my
dick can be." He placed a hand on the back of
her thigh and slid it beneath the hem of her
skirt, right toward her panties. "Sweet little
whispers and this pussy is all mine."

She laughed at his arrogance. "So, now
you're the pussy whisperer?"

"Hmmm. We'll have to test the theory when
I have you naked and my mouth is between
your legs."

The erotic mental image that popped into
her mind made her squirm on his shoulder.
"Not gonna happen unless you *put me down*."

He gave a long-suffering sigh but finally
bent over and let her heels touch the ground
again just as they reached the door leading to
the outside world, then let her have a second to
find her balance. When her head stopped
spinning, she tugged her skirt back down her

thighs and gave him a mock glare that told him he'd be lucky if he got anywhere near her girly bits for that stunt.

"Oh, don't go getting all prissy on me, Minx." Sexy humor darkened his gorgeous blue eyes. "Because I'm *so* whispering to your pussy tonight."

Truthfully, she couldn't wait to hear what he had to say.

WES FINISHED UPLOADING his newest listing for a luxury penthouse located at Legacy at Millennium Park, the asking price a cool ten million, then leaned back in his leather chair with a satisfied smile. He'd made a sale on a home in Lincoln Park earlier that morning, and a few hours ago the sellers of the penthouse he'd just posted had signed the agreement to use Premier Realty to broker the property. All in all, not terribly bad for a day's work.

He glanced at his wristwatch, noting the time. Five fifteen in the afternoon, and he was suddenly aware of the fact that he hadn't heard from Natalie all day, not by phone, text, or email. After last night's marathon of hot make-up sex for his barbaric attitude at the networking event—and testing his newfound pussy whispering skills, where he'd discovered that Natalie's naughty kitty cat loved when he talked dirty to it—he'd slipped out of her place at almost midnight, leaving her satisfied, beautifully disheveled, and smiling from the multiple orgasms her pussy had enjoyed. His dick had been equally happy and pleased with the evening's outcome.

He figured they'd both just had a busy day, with no down time for chitchat or smexy texts. But now that the rest of his evening was free, he wanted to spend it with Natalie, especially since they only had three more days left together.

Only three more days. That realization made an inexplicable sense of dread settle in his chest like a heavy weight. He absently rubbed the spot right above his heart, the one that told him just how difficult letting go of her was going to be. More so than any other woman who'd warmed his bed. And not just because of the phenomenal sex they had. No, he was going to miss those sweet and sexy smiles that were just for him. Her humor and her smart mouth. How she didn't let him get away with shit, and she had no qualms about calling him out on his boorish behavior. No other woman had ever come close to challenging him the way that Natalie did, and he never thought he'd ever admit it, but he actually *liked* her unpredictable personality.

But the fact remained that they'd both agreed to a casual affair, and she'd been straightforward about him being her transition guy. The guy who would sex her up for two weeks, then watch her walk away to find a man more capable of offering her a committed relationship than he would ever be. It shouldn't have bothered him—Jesus, he was a fucking pro at no-strings-attached sex—but it brought back those feelings of inadequacy and not being quite good enough.

And he hated it.

He exhaled a harsh breath, refusing to let old, bitter memories resurface. Instead, he picked up his cell phone and tapped out a playful text to Natalie.

Chinese food for dinner tonight at my place at seven? I want to show you all the clever things I can do with chopsticks. He followed that up with a winking emoticon, and hit send.

A few minutes later, she replied. *Ugh. Not unless you want me to barf.*

He frowned. Okay, not the response he was

expecting. *Care to explain what you mean so I don't take your comment personally?* He added a smiley face and forwarded the text.

The bubbles on the screen told him she was in the process of typing out an answer, and he waited patiently for the message.

I'm sorry. I either ate something yesterday that didn't agree with me or I caught a twenty-four-hour flu bug. I woke up at five this morning puking my guts out and I've been home in bed all day. Three barfing emoticons followed that statement. *I look and feel like something the cat dragged in. Like roadkill.* She included a skeleton face with two x's over its eyes.

The picture she painted wasn't a pretty one, but it made him chuckle. While most women would have explained the situation a bit more . . . delicately, Natalie didn't bother sugarcoating the truth. Bold and to the point, that was his girl.

Shaking his head, he moved his thumbs quickly over his phone's keyboard, grinning as he typed. *Why don't I bring over something that sounds good that you'd like to eat and won't test your gag reflexes? We can watch Netflix and chill. And by chill, I really do mean chill. It's not code for sex, I swear.*

He waited a good thirty seconds before her next text came through. *Did you not read the part of my text that said I look and feel like roadkill? Trust me, I'm not exaggerating. Thank you for the offer, but I'll be fine. I'm feeling much better than I was this morning.*

He felt bad that he hadn't checked in with her sooner, that she'd been home all day sick. Reluctantly, he sent a response. *Okay, then. I'll talk to you later.*

As soon as he dispatched the text, he regretted it. It really didn't matter how she looked, only that she'd had a crappy day and he wanted to do something to make her feel better.

And that's what motivated his next actions.

NATALIE WAS CURLED up in bed, hugging a pillow to her chest as she watched back-to-back rerun episodes of the now defunct *Friends* sitcom, her body feeling as though it had been through a boxing match—and lost. Every once in a while, she'd chuckle at Joey's stupid antics on the show, which told her she was definitely on the mend.

The worst of her nausea had passed—and no, she wasn't pregnant—along with the raging headache that had been pounding in her head most of the day. Her abdominal cramps were completely gone, though her muscles still ached. Her empty stomach had grumbled hungrily a few times, and when she thought of ingesting something, she no longer felt like she wanted to throw up. Except she just didn't have the *oomph* to get up, go to the kitchen, and make something to eat, though she knew she'd eventually have to.

A while later, a loud knock sounded at her door, followed by her cell phone buzzing with a text. She read the incoming message first, which was from Wes.

Let me in. I'm here to take care of you.

Natalie rolled to her back and groaned. As thoughtful as the gesture was, she really wasn't in the mood for company. She was in her rattiest pair of sweat pants and an old cotton T-shirt, and her hair was pulled back into a ponytail because she didn't want it getting in the way of her bending over the toilet earlier. She'd only recently had the energy to brush her teeth, but that didn't make up for her ghastly appearance. She couldn't remember looking or feeling worse than she did today, and this flu's dreadful aftermath was not an impression she wanted to leave in Wes's head.

Don't bother ignoring me. I'm not going away. And if you don't open the door in two minutes, I'm calling Connor to come over with his key to make sure you're still alive in there, and then you'll have two of us to deal with.

"Goddamn it," she muttered to herself. He'd actually pulled the brother card. No way did she want Connor here, too.

Come on, Minx. I even brought you your favorite Ben & Jerry's for when you feel better later. Chocolate Fudge Brownie.

The man was resorting to bribery, and despite herself, she smiled. *Okay. Fine. But I'm only opening the door because you have B&J's.* It had nothing to do with the man himself, she thought, trying to convince herself of the lie.

Getting out of bed, she shuffled through the living room in her fuzzy socks and made her way to the door. She checked the peephole and saw him grinning on the other side, looking so hot and sexy and full of himself, and damn if just *seeing* him didn't lift her spirits and make butterflies take flight in her stomach—and yes, they *were* butterflies. After today, she had intimate knowledge of the difference between a fluttering sensation and intestinal pain.

She opened the door, speaking before he could. "You *really* didn't have to do this."

"I know. I *really* wanted to," he teased right back, but then grew serious as his dark blue eyes searched her face. "I wanted to see for myself that you're okay."

She swallowed hard, so not used to this kind, caring side to Wes when they'd spent so many years butting heads and antagonizing one another—and most recently, the past eleven days getting naked as much as possible, in an attempt to fuck their attraction out of their systems. Unfortunately, for her, Wes was even more entrenched in her heart than he'd been before.

"I told you I was going to be fine," she said, suddenly self-conscious as she played with the hem of her faded T-shirt. "I look and feel gross, and I wasn't expecting company."

"You don't look that bad," he said, and grinned. "Not even close to roadkill."

She rolled her eyes. "You're such a liar, but I appreciate you sugarcoating the truth."

"I wasn't. You always look beautiful to me." And to prove his point, he leaned toward her and placed a soft, achingly sweet kiss on her cheek, as if she hadn't spent the day hurling up her toenails.

Her throat closed up with emotion, and because she wasn't able to talk past that knot in her vocal chords, she stepped back and opened the door wider for him to enter. He was holding two plastic grocery bags, one in each hand, and he took them into the kitchen with her following.

He started unloading the items onto the counter . . . canned soup, crackers, applesauce, Gatorade, a small pack of chamomile tea bags, and as promised, a pint of her favorite Ben & Jerry's ice cream. She wasn't quite ready to indulge in the latter, but the soup was beginning to sound really good.

"What can I do to help?" she asked automatically.

He started searching through cupboards, found a small pan, and set it on her stovetop. "You can go prop yourself up in bed with some pillows, make yourself comfortable, and wait for me to bring you your dinner. Oh, and you can get started on drinking this Gatorade to make sure you're hydrated." He pressed a chilled bottle of the drink into her hand.

It felt weird being doted on, and he must have seen the indecision on her expression because he pointed a finger toward her bed-room door and gave her a strict order. "Go. Now."

Knowing what he was capable of when he was in one of his bossy moods, she did as she was told. In her bedroom, she fluffed the bigger pillows up against the headboard, settled onto the mattress with the covers pulled up to her lap, and took a few sips of her drink.

By the time she'd finished watching the epi-sode of *Friends* she'd paused when she went to answer her door, Wes walked in with a steaming bowl of the chicken soup and a plate of crack-ers. He gave her a dishtowel to hold beneath the hot bowl so she didn't burn her hands and placed the saltines on the nightstand next to her Gatorade. Then he walked around the bed to the other side, toed off his shoes, and made himself comfortable beside her with the extra pillows stacked behind him. She'd never seen him fully clothed in her bed before, and oddly enough, it seemed more intimate than him being completely naked.

She swallowed a spoonful of the delicious soup, then glanced at him, her face warming when she caught him looking right back at her. "Wes . . . thank you for the food, but you don't have to stay." She was sure he had things he'd rather be doing than tending to her.

"I know I don't *have* to." He picked up the remote and pointed it at the TV and started pressing buttons. "We're going to watch Netflix and chill, like I told you. And by 'chill,' I mean relax. Do you want to watch another episode of *Friends*, or something else?"

He looked like he genuinely wanted to stay, and she was finding it difficult to argue when *she* wanted him to stay. "Whatever *you* want." The least she could do was let him pick the show or movie.

A slow, sinful grin eased up the corners of that gorgeous, talented mouth of his. "I guess watching porn is out of the question tonight, huh?" he asked, just as she put another spoonful of soup into her mouth.

She almost snorted a noodle out of her nose for swallowing and laughing at the same time, and he chuckled, too. God, she wasn't supposed to be laughing after the rotten day she'd had, but it felt good. And oddly normal with Wes. "Porn is definitely not an option tonight."

"Can't blame a guy for asking," he teased as he winked at her, then returned his attention to the catalog of movies he had to pick from.

He ended up choosing *Ferris Bueller's Day Off*, surprising her.

"I love this movie," she said, though it had been a while since she'd seen it.

"Me, too," he said, giving her a quick smile before pressing the play button. "With *Elf* coming in a close second."

"Yeah, they're total classics that are underappreciated these days." She munched on a saltine cracker, realizing just how grateful her stomach was to finally have something in it.

He nodded in agreement, then spouted off one of the movie's most iconic quotes. "*Life moves pretty fast. If you don't stop and look around once in a while, you could miss it.*"

His gaze was locked on hers, and after the sentences left his mouth, he looked at her, *really* looked at her, as if he was truly seeing her for the first time. Or seeing her for the first time in a whole different light than the frenemy she'd always been, based on Ferris Bueller's wise words. He wasn't gazing at her sexually or with lust but with the kind of emotion that went so much deeper than just a physical connection. The kind of emotion that would have made her weak in the knees had she been standing. As it was, her heart was knocking around in her chest, and it took more willpower than she possessed to break eye contact with him and let the moment fade.

They were both quiet as the movie started and she finished her soup and crackers and drank more of her Gatorade. After a while he paused the show, then took her bowl and plate to the kitchen, and she heard him cleaning up and washing dishes. When he returned, he turned off her bedroom light, got back into bed beside her, and scooched down a bit on the mattress so he wasn't totally upright.

He patted the space next to him, his smile affectionate. "Come here, Minx, so I can cuddle with you."

God, she loved that pet name, and she was going to miss hearing it once they went their separate ways. "You're not worried about catching my cooties if it's the flu?" she asked, certain he'd change his mind after the reminder of how sick she'd been.

He shook his head, not looking the least bit concerned. "Nah. I'll totally risk it for you."

Such simple words, but they made her melt inside. After readjusting the pillows, she snuggled up to his side and rested her head right where his chest tapered into his shoulder. He wrapped his arm around her, and she placed a hand on his abdomen—wishing he wasn't wearing his shirt—and relaxed one of her legs over his. They were tangled together in the best possible way, and while she thought he might feel too smothered and he'd want his space, it never happened.

So, Wes was a cuddler, she thought with a smile as she fixed her gaze on the movie they were watching. And a really good one. And he smelled amazing, too. Warm and masculine, the scent of him was both arousing and comforting, and she had to resist the urge to burrow closer, deeper, so she could memorize everything about this moment and this man and how something so simple as bringing her soup when she was sick made her feel so . . . special.

She couldn't remember the last time that a man she was in a relationship with had gone out of his way, above and beyond what was ex-pected, to take care of her. To just be with her. No pretenses of anything else. No expectations.

The one big thing she'd discovered in their two weeks together was that cocky, arrogant Wes Sinclair with the panty-dropping smile had a soft side he'd kept to himself. Until now.

He had all the makings of being perfect,

swoon-worthy boyfriend material, except he didn't want the commitment that came with it.

And that was a deal breaker for her.

Chapter Fifteen

"SO, WHEN ARE you going to tell Wes about the job offer in Atlanta?" Richard asked right before he lifted his Manhattan cocktail to his lips and took a sip.

Natalie sighed as she absently rubbed away the condensation on her glass of soda water, garnished with a lemon wedge. After being sick all day yesterday, she'd gone back to work today, but she wasn't ready to test her stomach with alcohol. But when Richard found out that she wouldn't be spending the evening with Wes like she'd normally been doing over the past two weeks, he'd coerced her into going to the Popped Cherry with him for a drink.

She was kind of bummed that Wes had to cancel any plans he might have made with her for tonight, their last night together, but she understood his reasons. A wealthy client of his from New York had unexpectedly flown into town for the day to view a piece of property he was interested in purchasing, and the visit had turned into a business dinner to discuss negotiations.

He'd texted her throughout the day to see how she was feeling, which she thought was sweet, and she appreciated his concern and his sexy and humorous messages. They'd made her smile and laugh . . . and also made her realize just how much she was going to miss him after tomorrow, when she no longer had a reason to see or talk to him on a daily basis. Who would have ever thought she'd feel that way about a man who'd once irritated the hell out of her?

"Hello?" Richard said wryly, bringing her thoughts back to the present and the way her friend looked a little miffed that her mind had wandered. "Are you even listening to me, or am I talking to myself?"

"I'm sorry." She shook her head and focused on him. "Yes, I'm listening."

He exhaled an exasperated breath. "Well, when are you going to tell Wes?" he asked again. "Or are you not going to tell him at all?"

She still hadn't made a final decision on the Atlanta job, but she was definitely leaning in that direction. Initially, she'd seen it as a positive career move and a great asset for her resume, but she'd always had reservations about leaving her family to go and live somewhere that was completely new to her. But currently, it was sort of a blessing in disguise, because now that her feelings for Wes had changed, living in another state would give her a fresh start. She wouldn't have to see him all the time. Wouldn't have to feel like she'd been stabbed in the heart every time she heard about his escapades with other women.

"Yes, I'm going to tell him," she pushed out, despite how much the words hurt. "There just hasn't been a good time to bring it up yet."

Richard smirked. "Obviously, great sex has been a priority."

Not so much a priority but a welcome and pleasurable distraction to the alternative of discussing her job offer with Wes. To keep her emotions from spilling over and crowding their way into their temporary affair.

Oh, wait. That had happened anyway.

God, she sucked at having flings—no pun intended. She'd always been a relationship kind of girl and that hadn't changed, nor had her dreams for her future. It just wasn't going to happen with Wes, so there was no sense in dragging out the inevitable.

"Tomorrow," she said, trying to sound more determined than she felt. "I'll tell him tomorrow once the bet is done."

It was a fitting way to end their affair, as well.

TODAY IS THE final day of our bet and your last opportunity to take advantage of my services. Anything come to mind?

Wes grinned as he read the text from Natalie, though the message was like a punch to the stomach and a squeeze to his dick at the same time. A punch because she'd brought up the fact that it was their final day together and a squeeze because his fantasies when it came to her were endless. And after nearly two days apart due to their conflicting schedules, he was excited to see her. Quite the novelty for him.

While most women bored him after a few dates, this woman did the exact opposite. Every time they were together, there was not only heat and attraction but a deeper connection between them that went beyond sexual tension. He'd realized the night at her place when she was sick and they'd just lain in her bed watching *Ferris Bueller's Day Off*, laughing and cuddling together, that what they shared might have started out as a sexfest, but it had morphed into a compatible, intimate relationship that, scarily enough, made him want . . . more.

The fact that he wanted to continue their monogamous relationship should have panicked him, but for the first time in his life, being with a woman felt . . . right. Like he'd found a piece of himself that had been missing, and he never wanted to be without again.

He just wasn't sure if she felt the same way, and God, the thought of her saying no to more than just sex, to rejecting anything other than an affair with him made his belly roil with nerves and apprehension. He was good enough to fuck . . . but was he good enough for her to date?

Shoving those troubling thoughts from his mind, he leaned back in his leather chair and tapped out a reply. *What kind of services are you offering, Minx?* There was innuendo all over that question. Deliberately, of course.

She didn't hesitate with her answer. *Anything*

and everything.

So many filthy, dirty thoughts played through his mind, but he kept his request simple and PG-rated. For now. *Well, for starters, I'd like you to pick up my dry cleaning and bring it to me here at the office.*

Hmmm . . . The one word was filled with disappointment, and her next message conveyed those feelings. *Not quite what I was expecting, but your wish is my command. I won't be able to get there until six, is that okay? I'm meeting a client at five for a walk-through and can stop by after that.*

Actually, that was perfect for what he had in mind. *That's fine, since everyone in the office will be gone by then. Which brings me around to the second thing I want . . . You. On my desk. Panties off, legs spread, and my cock deep inside your pussy.* It was a fantasy he'd entertained too many times to count over the years with Natalie in the starring role, and now that he had the chance, he wanted it to be reality.

Sounds like a fantastic way to end the bet. She added a cute little devilish emoticon to the end of the sentence.

End of the bet . . . end of them. The less-than-appealing words in Wes's head mocked him and tapped into those fucking insecurities he hated so much. He didn't want *anything* to end with Natalie, but her last text sounded as though she was having no issues with the end to their fling. And him.

I'll see you in a few hours, he texted back, then set his phone on his desk and scrubbed his hand down his face. Frustration and uncertainties wreaked havoc with his emotions, and he didn't know how to deal with the feelings, because he'd never been in this situation with a woman before. He was fucking inept and inadequate when it came to relationships, so did he really have anything to offer Natalie?

His cell phone buzzed, and he picked it up again, swiped it open, and read the message from Natalie.

I thought I'd get a head start on things and give you something to think about until I get there . . .

A photo popped up next, of pale pink silk-and-lace panties dangling from Natalie's fingertips, and he groaned. Judging by the narrow piece of fabric and thin strings it was attached to, he immediately knew that she was wearing one of those tight skirts that drove him fucking crazy. Hell, his dick was already half-hard just thinking about her walking around for the rest of the day without any underwear on.

He tapped out a quick reply with his thumbs. *You're going to pay for that.*

Oh, I hope so. I definitely think a spanking is in order, don't you?

He let out a strangled laugh as he sent a text back. *Hell fucking yeah. My palm is already itching to smack your ass until it's nice and pink.* God, he'd met his match, in ways he didn't even know were possible. In the most unexpected person and in the most unexpected way.

Their conversation ended, and he immersed himself in work for the rest of the afternoon, which was easy to do since he had a dozen different things on his plate that he needed to get done. Emails. Previewing properties and listings and their online inventory. Signing contracts and documents and leases. Following up on phone calls that needed to be returned.

At ten after five, his secretary popped her head into his office to let him know she was leaving. Max stopped by a few minutes after that and asked if he wanted to go for a drink, which Wes declined, stating he had some things to get caught up on. For the next twenty minutes, Wes listened as the rest of the employees left the building, until everything went quiet.

The following thirty minutes as he waited

for Natalie to arrive were the slowest of the day. He took off his suit coat and hung it up and rolled up his shirt sleeves. He completely cleared off the surface of his desk so there'd be nothing to get in the way of Wes fucking her on it as he'd promised. But with every second that passed, his anticipation grew, as did that little ball of nerves in his stomach as he tried to figure out the best way to ask Natalie if she wanted to date him exclusively. Shockingly, the thought didn't make him break out in a cold sweat. He wanted a chance to figure out what was between them beyond the bet that had put their attraction into motion.

Unless he was really and truly nothing more than her transition guy and she was ready to move on to someone more emotionally able to give of himself and provide what she needed?

Too many questions without any answers. Too many uncertainties that left him feeling restless and fearful that the one woman he truly wanted for more than just a fuck buddy didn't feel the same way.

For the first time in his adult life, he was standing in the shoes of all the women who'd wanted more from *him* over the years, while he'd ended things easily and walked away without any regrets. But now he was afraid that he'd be the one left in the dust and picking up the pieces of his . . . shattered heart. *Fuck.*

He squeezed his eyes shut and sent up a silent prayer. *Please, Karma, don't come back around and kick me in the balls for all my past insensitive behavior with women. I swear, Natalie is the only one who matters, and I don't want to lose her.*

The sound of the main door opening out in the reception area had Wes abruptly standing up behind his desk, his pulse racing with a tangle of nerves . . . until she came into view and everything in his orbit, in this office, calmed as if she belonged there. She walked in, his suits and shirts from the dry cleaners folded neatly over her arm in plastic bags, and hung the laundry on his coatrack just inside his office.

"Close and lock the door," he ordered huskily. It didn't matter that it was after hours and no one was around. He wasn't taking any chances that someone might walk in on what was about to happen.

He'd thought they'd talk first, but the second he saw Natalie, he suddenly wanted her with a fierce hunger that clawed at his insides and made him want to do that stake-his-claim-and-possess-every-inch-of-her thing again that had ended in burning-hot, uncivilized sex. His dick was already throbbing for her, his lust rising, matching the thickening of his cock.

With a raised brow, she did as he asked, securing them inside the office, then started toward him, wearing a hip-skimming, ass-hugging skirt, a pretty button-up silk blouse, and heeled pumps. All professional and proper on the outside and a fucking temptress on the inside.

He lifted his gaze to her beautiful face, taking in the blue eyes that were already dark with desire. He couldn't read her expression, but right now, in this moment, it didn't matter what was going on in her mind. She knew what she was walking into. She'd tempted the beast the moment she'd slipped her panties off and sent him a picture of her holding them.

By the time she came around to his side of the desk, his entire body was vibrating with the need to have her. It took supreme effort not to just push her back on his cleared-off desk and take her like a rutting animal—because that's what she did to him. Made him feel wild and aggressive and so desperate to be inside of her he could barely think straight.

She blinked at him, much too innocently,

and one side of his mouth curled up in a sinful smile. "You know what I want, baby," he murmured in a low, commanding tone. "You know what I'm waiting for."

Biting her sexy lower lip, she turned around, shimmied the hem of her skirt up over her hips to her waist, then bent over his desk with her hands braced on top. Her back was arched so sensually, her ass smooth and bare as she looked over her shoulder at him, her gaze heavy-lidded with heat and a forbidden anticipation.

"Spank me, Wes."

She was waiting for him to play out this fantasy however he wanted, giving him all the control. He stroked his palm over one soft, pale cheek, and when she least expected it, he gave the one side a sharp, stinging slap that made her gasp, then moan for more.

"Such a naughty, naughty Minx." *His* minx, he thought possessively, and landed another smack to the other mound. Her skin turned warm and pink, her thighs quivered, and when he slid his fingers between her legs, he exhaled on a harsh moan as he was greeted with her silky-soft, slick arousal. He swore louder when he slid two fingers inside her and she bucked back against his hand.

Abruptly, he turned her around and pushed her back so that she was sitting on his desk, her skirt still bunched around her waist, her legs spread apart just enough for him to glimpse the soft, swollen folds of her sex. He wanted to drop to his knees and worship her like she deserved, but suddenly, they were both pulling at each other's clothes, the urgency between the two of them like an unstoppable hurricane gathering force.

He nearly ripped open her blouse in his haste to unfasten the buttons, but once they were undone, he shoved the material and her bra straps down her arms until her breasts spilled free—while she impatiently unbuckled his belt, unzipped his pants, and pushed them down his thighs so they were out of the way. His mouth landed on her breasts, sucking, licking, and biting both nipples. She gripped his aching shaft, stroking the length in her palm. Her thumb found the drop of pre-come beading on the tip and used it to lubricate the head.

He gritted his teeth and fumbled to get his wallet out of his pants to retrieve the condom he'd stashed there for a moment like this, and sheathed himself in record time. He hooked his arms around the backs of her knees so that they were draped over the crook of his elbows and spread her legs wide. He gripped her hips in his hands to hold her still, because once he was inside her, he knew there would be no holding back the urgency to make her his in every way imaginable.

"Put my cock where you want it," he demanded in a voice that sounded as rough and gritty as sandpaper. "Where I fucking *need* it."

She whimpered anxiously and guided the crown of his shaft through her slick folds, bathing it in her slippery heat until he was poised at the entrance to her body. He pushed in, penetrating that tight opening just a few inches while Natalie flattened her hands behind her on the desk, as if knowing to brace herself for his first brutal thrust inside her.

With a hard jerk of his hips, he slammed so deep she cried out and he shuddered from the jarring impact before he started moving in earnest, the rhythm hard and fast and out of control. She felt like coming home, like fucking bliss—and he wasn't the kind of guy who waxed poetic about sex. But this ... being inside of Natalie was sublime, and he *knew* without any doubts that nothing else would ever compare.

His eyes traveled from where they were joined so intimately and moved upward, taking in the way her naked breasts bounced with every brutal stroke and the beautiful flush that swept up her neck and colored her cheeks. Her lips were parted, and he locked his gaze onto hers so that she could see exactly what she did to him, how she drove him to the brink, and how much he *needed* her.

He was beyond desperate for her to feel the same.

He powered back into her, knowing by her soft gasp that the exquisite ache building inside of him wasn't just one-sided. But he wanted verbal proof, needed her to acknowledge it, too.

"Feel that, Natalie?" he rasped, the punishing pace of his thrusts ensuring she'd be sore for the next day. "Feel me inside of you? Fucking you? Filling you, over and over?"

Her eyes glazed over with ecstasy. "Yes. Oh, God, yes," she whispered, the slight catch to her voice telling him that she was as close to climaxing as he was.

"I want to hear you scream my name when you come," he ordered, doubling his efforts to push her over the edge, his cock so hard and thick he knew the magnitude of his release was going to supersede all others. "Nobody is here, baby. It's just you and me and *this*."

As if he'd given her permission to let loose, she chased after her orgasm, and he watched and felt as it swept her up in its fury and she screamed his name so loudly it made his ears ring with the passionate, uninhibited sound.

The perfect, wet silk of her pussy clasping his cock and the openly vulnerable look in her eyes made him weak in the knees. The connection between them went beyond the physical, and he felt as though he'd been stripped bare, his heart no longer just his. The sight of Natalie giving herself over to him so willingly caused his own climax to surge through him, the hot rush of it so fucking powerful it stole the breath from his lungs and made him collapse on top of her in a heap.

His face was buried in the crook of her neck, and they were both breathing hard. Eventually, he lifted his head and smiled down at her, and while she returned the gesture, there was a guarded look in her eyes that reminded him why she was here, or why she *thought* she was here . . . to indulge in one last tryst and to end their two-week bet.

They needed to talk, but he needed a moment . . . to get rid of the condom and to clear his head so he could think straight. He moved away from her and helped her down from the desk, and she immediately tugged the hem of her skirt to cover herself, the euphoria they'd both just enjoyed quickly dissipating. He could see and feel her emotionally withdrawing, replacing the smart-alecky, straightforward woman he'd spent the last two weeks with, and had fallen hard for, with a far too serious demeanor.

"I'll be right back, so don't go anywhere," he said lightly, trying to keep calm until he figured out what was going on with her.

He went into the bathroom that adjoined his office and quickly cleaned up, washed his hands, and tucked everything back in. When he returned, he half expected her to be gone, but thank God, she was still there. She was no longer behind his desk. She'd moved over to the windows overlooking the city, her arms crossed over her chest as if she was trying to protect herself from something, but he had no idea *what*.

He joined her, hating the tangible walls she'd put up. She was probably preparing herself for him to end things, as they'd agreed—*as he'd always dealt with his relationships*—but it was the furthest thing from what he had in mind. He'd just spent the absolute *best* two weeks with a woman he'd known for most of his life. His best friend's little sister, his business adversary, his frenemy, and the thought of dating her exclusively for the foreseeable future didn't make him break out in hives. In fact, it made him feel . . . complete.

He quietly exhaled a deep breath. "Natalie . . . I was hoping we could talk."

She shook her head, and when her gaze met his, his gut twisted at the sadness he saw glimmering in the depths. "Actually, there's something I need to tell you first."

Whatever she had to say, he suddenly didn't want to hear it, because his entire body was telling him to brace for the worst. But even if she believed they were through, he still had the chance to change her mind about them, right?

"Okay," he said, shoving his hands deep into the front pockets of his slacks. *Ladies first and all that.*

"A few weeks ago, a recruiter contacted me about a position with a high-profile realty firm in Atlanta that was interested in hiring me, based on my current portfolio," she said. "It's a small, privately owned company with room for advancement and great benefits, and it's exactly the kind of move I'm looking to make in my career. I'm letting them know on Monday that I'm taking the job."

He felt blindsided, though he shouldn't have been. She'd always been honest about her aspirations, in business and with her desire to be in a committed relationship with a man that led to marriage and babies—which he'd blatantly scorned that night they'd discussed his parents' marriage and subsequent nasty divorce.

With every word she spoke, his confidence spiraled and his hopes dwindled. A job offer wasn't something he could compete with—hell, he'd already turned down her desire to work for Premier Realty—and why would she stay with him, a player with no real track record with women, when she'd been offered a sure thing? Yeah, he'd gone into this affair knowing he was her transition guy, but fuck, it hurt.

"When?" he asked, forcing the question out.

"In about a month," she replied softly, a sudden moisture in her eyes. "I'll need time to pack up and move, to sell my place . . ."

Don't go. The plea got stuck in his throat, not

because he was afraid to speak the words but because he knew he didn't have the right to ask her to stay.

"They'll be lucky to have you," he said instead, and could have sworn she flinched at what he'd meant as a compliment.

"Thanks." She gave him a half-hearted smile, her voice tight with the unshed tears he saw in her eyes. "I need to go."

When she turned around and walked away, he didn't try and stop her, but his aching heart *knew* she was taking a piece of him with her. That he'd never be the same once she walked out of his office, out of his life.

She opened the door and gasped in shock to find her brother, Connor, standing out in the hallway. As soon as he saw his sister and what was probably anguish on her face, his own expression turned protective . . . and fucking furious.

"Natalie, what's wrong?" he asked gruffly.

She shook her head. "Nothing," she said, but her cracking voice said otherwise. "I'm fine."

She brushed past Connor and her brother watched her go with a concerned frown. Once she was out of the building, Connor turned his head and pinned Wes with a near violent stare that was just as livid as his next words.

"What the *fuck* is going on?"

Chapter Sixteen

WES STOOD HIS ground as Connor stalked into his office, his shirt and jeans stained with dirt and grime from working on one of their properties they were flipping, his jaw clenched tight with anger. He stopped in front of Wes, his gaze blazing with displeasure and another sentiment that looked very much like betrayal.

The first emotion Wes could have dealt with. The second one was far more difficult to digest and made him feel like complete and utter shit. Connor was his best friend, and had been since before they were even teenagers. He was the guy who'd always had his back in any given situation, and there was no doubt in Wes's mind that Connor trusted Wes implicitly.

He had a horrible, awful feeling he'd fucked that all to hell, and might not have only lost Natalie but possibly Connor's friendship, as well, all in one fell swoop.

"You did it, didn't you?" Connor demanded, gaze narrowed and his voice heated. "You fucking slept with my sister, the one woman I'd expect you to keep your dick *out* of. Was screwing around with Natalie part of your requirement for her to fulfill the terms of your bet?"

Irritation tightened across Wes's shoulders, but he let his friend get everything off his chest before he answered, telling himself that Connor, as Natalie's big brother, had the right to defend his sister's honor. Even though they'd done nothing wrong.

"Yes, we slept together and no, it wasn't a requirement," he replied, glaring at Connor for him even thinking that Wes would stoop to that level. "Everything about it was consensual." He wasn't about to inform Connor that *Natalie* had suggested the affair. It didn't matter at this point, because they both had agreed.

Connor jabbed a finger toward the door. "Then why the hell did she just leave here looking fucking devastated?"

Wes wasn't sure he had an answer to that. *He* hadn't ended the fling, *she* had. And she was accepting a great job in Atlanta with an upscale firm that was everything she claimed she was working toward, so he didn't understand why she'd be crushed by the end to their affair. Wasn't this what she wanted? A temporary fuck buddy before she *transitioned* into the next phase of her life?

Jesus Christ. He was so fucking confused.

"I need a drink," Wes muttered, and headed over to the wet bar in the corner of his office.

He retrieved two lowball glasses from the shelf and the bottle of Macallan single malt scotch he normally reserved for clients, usually to celebrate a sale or purchase. Today, he needed a shot to soothe his ego and his nerves, and Connor needed one to calm the fuck down so they could have a civilized conversation.

After pouring a liberal amount for each of them, he carried one of the glasses over to Connor and pressed it into his friend's hand. "Care to sit down and stay awhile?" Wes asked in a droll tone, and fully expected Connor to tell him to fuck off and die.

Surprisingly, Connor huffed out a breath, then settled his big body into one of the chairs in front of Wes's desk, while Wes sat down in his leather chair across from his friend. He didn't dare look at the desk itself because he knew he'd remember how beautiful Natalie had looked spread across the mahogany while his name fell from her lips not even a half hour ago, so instead he kept his gaze trained straight ahead at Connor.

The two of them stared each other down as they drank their scotch in moody silence, though Connor's gaze was far more intimidating. He figured the man would speak when he was good and ready.

Wes understood why Connor was so protective of his little sister. For one thing, growing up, he'd always been that way, but Wes knew this current anger stemmed from the fact that Connor had been the one to catch Natalie's douchebag of a boyfriend cheating on her. He'd been the one to tell his sister what he'd seen, and watched as she'd fallen apart. So yeah, when it came to men and his sister, Connor was definitely in protective big brother mode and had taken it upon himself to make sure anyone interested in her was good enough for Natalie.

Wes hated that Connor lumped him into the latter category and found him lacking.

Connor downed the rest of his liquor and set the glass on the desk with a loud, aggressive clack. Wes decided they'd spent enough time having a Mexican standoff, and now it was time to be the adults they were.

"You ready to discuss this rationally?" he asked, then finished his own drink and set his glass aside, not nearly as belligerently as Connor had. Wes wasn't interested in having a pissing contest. Honestly, he just needed someone to talk to about the situation, and he *really* wanted that person to be Connor, his best friend—*if* the other man could be level-headed about the situation.

"That depends on how much of an asshole you were to my sister," Connor said, deadpan.

So much for level-headed. "I wasn't an asshole, and I swear I didn't take advantage of her." Wes plowed his fingers through his hair in frustration and decided to lay everything out on the table. What the fuck did he have to lose at this point?

"We both agreed to the affair because we're attracted to each other, and yeah, it was supposed to be temporary and just for the duration of the bet. She wasn't looking for anything serious and neither was I."

Connor's gaze darkened with animosity again and his hands gripped the sides of the chair, but he kept quiet and let Wes continue explaining.

"But then . . . that changed and it wasn't about just the sex anymore."

Connor made a face at the insinuation of his sister getting it on with his best friend, and Wes *almost* laughed. God, he couldn't believe he was discussing his sex life and his feelings for Natalie with her brother. It was all kinds of wrong, but no way did he want Connor to think that his sister had been nothing more than a casual fuck. It was the furthest thing from the truth.

"There's always been this thing between me and Natalie, even when we were teenagers. We've always been competitive, and we've always butted heads and antagonized one another, but beneath all that, we were both attracted to each other and trying to act like we weren't."

"Yeah, no shit, Sherlock," Connor drawled sardonically. "Don't you think I didn't see that tension between the two of you every time you were in the same room together? It doesn't take a rocket scientist to see that both of you were

CARLY PHILLIPS & ERIKA WILDE

trying not to give in to temptation."

Wes rocked back in his chair, trying to process the knowledge that Connor had known all along. "Why didn't you say something to me?"

"Because I didn't want the two of you getting involved," he said bluntly. "Not because you're my best friend and she's my sister. I didn't want you to break her fucking heart, because that's what you do, Wes." He raised a brow, his gaze pointed and resentful. "But it looks as though that happened, anyway."

Wes didn't mind owning up to something that was his fault and he was responsible for, but he wasn't keen on taking the blame for something he didn't do. The only way Wes could have broken Natalie's heart was if *he'd* been the one to walk away. But that hadn't happened, and he wanted Connor to understand that.

"I know I don't have the best track record with women." As soon as the statement was out of his mouth, he laughed dryly and shook his head. "Hell, I don't even *have* a track record when it comes to relationships, because I've never let myself get involved longer than a few dates. That's the way I've always been, so I get why you think I'm the bad guy. But just to clear

260

things up, ending this . . . *relationship*," he said, because what he'd shared with Natalie had been more than just an affair or fling to him, "was Natalie's idea, not mine. If I had my choice, we'd still be together, officially as a couple. But clearly that wasn't what your sister wanted."

Connor leaned forward in his chair and braced his forearms on his thighs, scrutinizing Wes a moment before speaking again. "Are you . . . in love with her?"

Wes gave the question serious considera-tion. He'd always had feelings for Natalie, and a few weeks ago, had he been posed with the same question, he would have said he *cared* for her. Because what the hell did he really know about love?

But what he felt for her now was so much more than just affection and caring and attrac-tion. Being with Natalie was like a powerful drug and the best kind of addiction. When he was with her, even lying in bed holding her when she was sick, he felt happy and content. And when they were apart, he was constantly thinking about her and how soon he could see her again. He wanted to make her happy. He loved fighting and arguing with her because she was so feisty and full of fire, and he loved that she wasn't afraid to stand up to him, to go toe-to-toe over something she believed in. And he hated how empty and quiet his house was when she wasn't in it.

But mostly, the thought of *not* having Natalie in his life was like a crushing blow to his heart.

"Yeah, I love her," he said, the words sounding rusty to his own ears. *But what if she didn't love him back?* The mere possibility made him feel as though he couldn't breathe.

Connor frowned at him, obviously seeing his panic-stricken expression and guessing at the source. "Look, I'm going to let you in on something, and if you ever tell Natalie I told you this, I will not only deny any knowledge of this next conversation but I will also kick you in the nuts so fucking hard you'll never have sex again."

Jesus, this was serious. "Okay," he said cautiously.

After hesitating a few seconds, Connor spoke. "When Natalie was nineteen, I read something I shouldn't have, and she would be *pissed* if she knew."

Wes was definitely intrigued.

"She was living at home and going to UIC,"

he continued, referring to the University of Illinois at Chicago, where she'd attended classes. "I was working on a construction site and stopped by after work to pick up something my mom still had packed away in my room, but no one was home. No big deal, I used my key to get in, and when I walked by Natalie's room, her door was open and I saw what looked like a book on her bed. But it was pink, and I thought that was odd, so I picked it up and flipped through it . . . and realized it was her journal."

Connor's face flushed and he shifted on his chair, and Wes almost smirked to see his friend so uncomfortable.

"I *know* I should have put it down and walked away . . . but I didn't." Connor's chagrin grew. "I was a dick and read some of the entries, and I just kept turning pages, because I couldn't believe what I was reading. Natalie was in love with you. Not a little-girl crush or a teenage infatuation, but judging by the words she wrote, it was the kind of love a woman feels toward a guy who means everything to her. You've *always* been that guy, Wes, and I'm pretty damn sure you still are."

Wes had no words. None. He was too blown away by what his friend just told him. He could easily rationalize that Connor reading the journal entry was a long time ago, that Natalie's feelings were no longer the same, that she'd dated other men and had a long-term serious relationship that could have led to marriage. But what did Wes expect? No woman was going to wait around for a guy who showed no signs of ever loving her back, and the easiest thing to do would be to move on and start fresh . . .

Just like Natalie was moving on to Atlanta and beginning a new life there. Was she taking the job because she believed he'd never be capable of giving her what she wanted? What she needed?

He met Connor's gaze. "Did you know about the job in Atlanta she was considering?"

"Yeah, she mentioned it." His friend shrugged a shoulder. "Given the choice, she would have been a great asset to this company, but you stated your reasons for not wanting to hire her on, and while I respected that decision, as did Max and Kyle, I didn't, and still don't, agree with it. That whole 'it's not smart to mix business with family' is a bunch of bullshit, and you know it."

His logic, at the time, had made total sense to Wes. It had everything to do with the emotional scars and the horrible memories of his parents' divorce. How family disputes, even in a business, could cause tension and resentments and tear relationships apart—because that's all he'd known. But being put in a situation where he stood to lose everything that was important to him—and the firm wasn't number one on the list, Natalie was—changed his whole perspective.

"So, now that you have an idea of how she feels about you, are you *really* going to let her go to Atlanta?" Connor asked, his gaze direct.

No. No, he wasn't. "I take it I have your blessing, as her brother and my best friend?"

"Yeah, you do," Connor said, the corners of his mouth lifting in a genuine smile. "I trust you with Natalie, and I know you'd never intentionally hurt her. And I know she's good for you, too, and that's what matters."

If Connor trusted him, Wes realized that he had to trust himself to be the man that Natalie wanted and needed in her life. He wasn't letting her go without a fight. Without laying all his cards on the table and making sure she knew, without any doubts, how he felt about her.

He had to try, because he knew if he didn't do everything in his power to make her stay, losing Natalie Prescott would be his biggest regret in life.

And he wasn't about to let that happen.

SATURDAY AFTERNOON, NATALIE was curled up on the couch, finally eating the Ben & Jerry's Wes had bought for her while watching *The Notebook* on Netflix. Stuffing her face with ice cream and watching one of the most tragic love stories to appear on the big screen was certainly an appropriate way to drown her sorrows and heartache.

After the many text messages she'd received that morning, she wasn't surprised when she heard a knock on the door. She'd been expecting the visitor, even though she had no desire to have company and had told him as much. Numerous times. But she also knew he wouldn't go away, either, and that's why she set down her carton of Chocolate Fudge Brownie and finally went to answer the door.

She opened it without looking through the peephole, and surprise, surprise, Richard stood on the other side. "I told you I'm a total grump and not in the mood to be social."

"Too fucking bad," he retorted, unfazed by

her cranky disposition as he walked right into her condo without an invitation, a bakery bag in his hand.

She sighed, closed the door, and followed him into the living room.

He eyed the carton of ice cream on the coffee table, then glanced at her with a raised brow. "I brought chocolate cake for the depressed and broken-hearted, but it looks like someone already beat me to it."

"Wes bought it for me when I was sick, when he brought over the soup," she admitted.

Richard grinned, looking impressed. "So, the guy *does* have potential."

She rolled her eyes because it didn't matter what Wes had done three days ago, the sweet gestures and taking care of her when she was sick, because all that was over. She'd gone into the affair knowing who Wes was, that there wouldn't be any promises, and she'd certainly known not to get more emotionally attached to him than she already was.

Too late for that, her heart mocked her.

Richard gave her clothes an admiring once-over. "By the way, I approve of your mopey attire. It's very . . . chic."

Okay, that made her laugh, damn him. The

oversized cable-knit sweater that came to her thighs and the matching knee-high knitted socks were far from chic, but they made her feel warm and cozy and comforted. She grabbed her ice cream, sat back down, and resumed play on her movie.

Richard grabbed the remote and hit pause.

She glared at him. "Hey, this is my pity party, and I can sulk and watch depressing movies if I want to."

He shook his head and put the remote out of her reach. "I wouldn't be a good friend if I didn't help you out of this slump. Let's go shopping and spend lots of money. Retail therapy can do wonders for a girl's morale."

"I don't want to go anywhere." She leaned her head back against the top of the couch and closed her eyes, hating the heavy, oppressive feeling in her chest that reminded her of everything that had happened the day before in Wes's office.

The hot sex she'd become addicted to, and the fact that Wes hadn't even batted an eye when she told him about moving to Atlanta. How he'd given her an aloof *they'll be lucky to have you* that had felt like a knife to her heart. He might as well have said, "Hey, it was nice fucking you. I'll see ya around."

She swallowed the lump forming in her throat, refusing to cry any more tears over Wes. Last night, she could have filled buckets, but just as she'd done after Mitch, she was going to move forward and figure things out, one day at a time. On her own and without Wes. And in Atlanta.

God, what made her think she could have a fling with Wes and remain unaffected? That she could keep her emotions out of the equation when she'd loved him for so many years? And why did it hurt so damn much that she hadn't heard a word from him since walking out of his office last night?

Because it's over, Natalie.

"Hey, you okay?" Richard asked, his concerned voice making her open her eyes again.

"Yes . . .no," she added truthfully as all the pain inside of her bubbled to the surface. "Everything about this situation sucks. I never should have suggested an affair with Wes, because my stupid heart doesn't know how to sleep with a guy and not get involved." She grabbed one of the throw pillows on the couch, set it on her lap, and gave it a frustrated punch. "Oh, who am I kidding? My heart was involved way before we had sex."

Richard gave her a sympathetic look. "Yesterday, when you saw Wes, did you tell him how you feel about him?"

"God, no." She was sure her horrified expression spoke for itself. "And make things even more awkward between us than they already will be? So he'll feel sorry for me for being in love with him for . . . way too fucking long? I've already been in a one-sided relationship and have no desire to go through that again."

"Whoa," Richard said, trying to settle her down. "I doubt there's any comparison."

No, there really wasn't, she admitted, slumping lower on the couch. She was just angry at herself for believing that things could be different between her and Wes. That the two of them were heading toward something more promising and intimate. That he'd take a chance on her, on them, and realize that all relationships didn't reflect that of his parents.

After a while, Richard let out a sigh. "Look, if we're not going to go out, then you're going to listen to what I have to say."

She gave him a wary look, wondering if she ought to grab her purse and drag him out the door so she didn't have to hear his lecture. "Then get it over with."

"Don't worry. I'll keep it quick and simple and to the point," he assured her. "Remember when I told you not to be so quick to walk away from something or someone that could mean more to you than a job?"

"And I believe I said Wes isn't that someone."

"I think he is," Richard refuted. "But he can't be that someone if he doesn't know how you feel. If you don't *tell* him how you feel. Don't let your fears possibly rob you of the man of your dreams. Because let's face it. That man *is* dreamy."

Natalie laughed and realized through her stubborn frustration that, yes, Richard was right. If she didn't open up and tell Wes what was in her heart, she would never know how it all might play out, and there was a fifty-fifty chance that they could get it right. Before she left for Atlanta, she owed it to herself to find out if her time with Wes truly was just a fling or if there was potential for something more, like a future together.

A knock sounded at the door, and Natalie groaned and dragged her fingers through her hair. "God, I hope that's not my brother. I managed to avoid Connor when I took the walk of shame out of Wes's office last night, but he knew something was wrong, and I figured it was only a matter of time before he'd start prying."

Another knock, and Richard got to his feet before she did. "I'll get it for you."

He walked to the door and looked out the peephole, then glanced back at her with a huge grin that both confused and worried Natalie.

"Who is it?" she asked.

"Mr. Big Shot," he said, and his delighted expression grew. "And I'm betting money that he's here because he came to his goddamn senses and realized that you are the best thing that's ever happened to him."

Natalie wasn't so sure, but she was definitely interested in what Wes had to say . . . and yes, she had something to tell him, as well.

WHEN THE DOOR to Natalie's condo opened, the last person Wes expected to see on the other side was Richard. And for the smallest, briefest moment, he experienced a jolt of possessiveness that stiffened his entire body— until he reminded himself that Richard was gay and had no interest in Natalie that way.

Thank God, because he wouldn't hesitate to fight to the death for what was his. Okay, *to the death* was extreme, but ever since his conversation with Connor last night, and coming to some insightful realizations about his own feelings for Natalie, Wes was prepared to do whatever it took to ensure that she knew she belonged to him and with him.

And seeing her standing behind Richard in the living room, looking beyond beautiful and like everything he'd never known he needed only cemented every feeling he had for her and every decision he'd made since she'd walked out of his office last night. Never again would she walk away from him with the intention of ending their relationship. He'd make damn sure of that.

"Hey, Wes, what brings you by?" Richard greeted him affably.

Wes switched his gaze back to the man in front of him, realizing by the amusement in his eyes that Richard was totally messing with him. He obviously knew what had happened between him and Natalie, so it was pretty clear what Wes was doing there. But just in case Richard needed him to spell it out, he did.

"I'm here to talk to Natalie," he said. "Privately, if you don't mind."

"Nope, don't mind at all," Richard replied and moved back to let him in. "She's all yours. Literally," he added with a knowing wink that helped Wes to gauge Natalie's frame of mind—and where she stood emotionally.

After giving the other man a grateful nod, Wes walked into the condo a few steps, then glanced back at Richard, only to find him blatantly staring at his ass. *Really?*

"Eyes up here, dude," Wes said, pointing to his face, though he wasn't at all offended but, rather, amused. "And you need to stop staring at my ass. It's not polite."

Richard laughed. "Damn, it's a really nice one. You two kids play nice," he said, then he was gone, closing the door behind him.

Wes looked back at Natalie, seeing the hope in her eyes that hit him square in the chest and made him realize what he'd almost lost for good. And it was that thought that prompted him to walk across the living room to her, and when he reached where she stood and she looked up at him with those big, gorgeous blue eyes, he didn't even hesitate to frame her jaw in his hands and tip her mouth up to his for a kiss.

The moment his lips touched hers, she moaned softly, her body swaying toward his, telling him everything he needed to know. She wanted him, just as much as he wanted and needed her. And Jesus, the knowledge almost brought him to his knees.

He had so much to tell her. So much to say, and even though it was one of the most difficult things he had to do, he ended the kiss. But he didn't let her go. He held on to her face, gently, tenderly. The vulnerable gleam in her eyes matched the one in his heart. A heart he'd never given to anyone before, and he was suddenly glad about that, because it only belonged to one person. This incredible woman who held it in the palm of her hand. Every part of it.

"Tell me, Minx," he said in a soft command as his thumbs stroked her cheeks. "Tell me what I want to hear. What I desperately need to know."

"Wes . . ." Her voice quivered with uncertainties.

He understood, and he sought to reassure her. "Trust me, baby. Take the leap. I'm here to catch you. I'll always be here to catch you. *Trust me.*"

He knew he was asking for a lot, and as he

stared into her eyes, he saw the greatest gift he knew he'd ever receive from this woman. It was confidence and exhilaration and a tenderness he wasn't quite sure he deserved but he'd do everything in his power to earn.

"I love you," she whispered, and Jesus, his heart fucking *soared*. "I love you so much, Wes Sinclair."

He didn't make her wait for his own leap of faith. "I love you, Natalie Prescott. More than I ever believed was possible."

She shook her head. "But you didn't say anything last night . . . "

He didn't mention that she'd withheld her feelings as well, because really, at this point, who cared? "You never gave me the chance. And once you told me about Atlanta, I thought you'd made up your mind and that I would be the last person you'd stay in Chicago for."

"You would be wrong," she said, placing her hands on his chest and leaning closer into him. "*Very* wrong."

"I've never been happier to be wrong," he teased as he pressed his forehead to hers, a happy smile curving his mouth. "And just so you know, being wrong doesn't happen often."

She laughed. "No, I imagine it doesn't."

He kissed her again, reveling in the open way she responded and the fact that he had endless days with her to enjoy more kisses. Daily kisses. Morning kisses and evening kisses. And even some in between, at work . . . Oh, yeah, *work*.

He lifted his head so he could look into her eyes, so she could see how serious he was. "You're staying right here in Chicago with me. And you're going to work at Premier Realty as a broker. I talked to all the guys earlier today, and we all agree that we want you there. It's stupid not having you work there, and I'll admit it was because of my personal insecurities. Which I swear we'll work through." That's why he hadn't come sooner. He'd had a meeting with the guys to ensure they were all on the same page. Or rather, for Wes to prove to friends that he'd finally pulled his head out of his ass and was making the right choice for the firm and not just himself.

Her eyes went wide, and she shook her head. "I don't need that," she insisted. "I only need you."

"You have me. Exclusively. And the deal is nonnegotiable."

Her smile was huge and intoxicating. "As long as you're part of the package, I accept."

"Oh, baby, I am." He swept her up into his arms and took her into the bedroom, where he pulled off that cable-knit sweater so he had access to all the creamy skin beneath.

He stripped off her bra and panties but made her leave those hot-as-fuck knee-high socks on her legs. Once he was completely naked, he joined her on the mattress, moving over her and settling right where he wanted to spend every single night for the rest of his days. In her bed. In her arms. Between her soft, welcoming thighs.

He braced his arms next to her head and looked into her eyes, already dark and needy with desire. All for him. They had so many more things to talk about. Details and plans for the future and figuring out how to make everything between them work. He knew it wouldn't always be easy and there would undoubtedly be obstacles for them to overcome. He expected there to be bumps in the road while the two of them navigated this relationship thing that was so new to him.

He was wholly committed to her, and they'd already established the most important thing between them, and that was being in love. The rest would come.

Thank you for reading BIG SHOT. We hope you enjoyed Wes and Natalie's story! We would appreciate it if you would help others enjoy this book by leaving a review at your preferred e-tailer. Thank you!

Up next, Max Sterling in FAKING IT.

Confirmed bachelor Max Sterling isn't into rescuing damsels in distress, but when the very tempting Hailey Ellison needs his help, there's only one thing for him to do. Step in and pose as her loving fiancé. Except there is nothing fake about his attraction to her, or how much he wants her beneath him in his bed, moaning his name. But what starts as a fun, flirty, temporary engagement quickly becomes something more serious that neither one ever anticipated.

Order FAKING IT today!

Sign up for Carly Phillips & Erika Wilde's Newsletters:

Carly's Newsletter
http://smarturl.it/CarlysNewsletter

Erika's Newsletter
http://smarturl.it/ErikaWildeNewsletter

ABOUT THE AUTHORS

CARLY PHILLIPS

Carly Phillips is the *N.Y. Times* and *USA Today* Bestselling Author of over 50 sexy contemporary romance novels featuring hot men, strong women and the emotionally compelling stories her readers have come to expect and love. Carly is happily married to her college sweetheart, the mother of two nearly adult daughters and three crazy dogs (two wheaten terriers and one mutant Havanese) who star on her Facebook Fan Page and website. Carly loves social media and is always around to interact with her readers. You can find out more about Carly at www.carlyphillips.com.

ERIKA WILDE

Erika Wilde is the author of the sexy Marriage Diaries series and The Players Club series. She lives in Oregon with her husband and two daughters, and when she's not writing you can find her exploring the beautiful Pacific Northwest. For more information on her upcoming releases, please visit website at www.erikawilde.com.